"You're the only one here who totally gets me and my concern for these animals. It'd mean a lot if you'd hike with me," Chance said.

Chance's life had been bereft of joy for the past six months. How could she consider denying him this one small pleasure?

"I, um, I'm not sure that—"

He smiled. "Please? For me?" He wove his arm through hers and slid his strong, warm hand down until their hands met palm-to-palm.

His touch branded in her a deep and irrefutable knowing.

This is meant to be.

Awestruck, she felt her heart leap inside her.

The world around the two of them faded away. All the personal protests and reasons she shouldn't ceased to exist in her mind. The chaos calmed.

All she could see was Chance.

Chance's face sent her pulse skittering. He gently drew her close. "Walk with me, Chloe?"

Her gaze welded to his, she felt a little dazed.

At this moment she w
to take that walk with

Books by Cheryl Wyatt

Love Inspired

*A Soldier's Promise
*A Soldier's Family
*Ready-Made Family
*A Soldier's Reunion
*Soldier Daddy
*A Soldier's Devotion
*Steadfast Soldier

*Wings of Refuge

CHERYL WYATT

An R.N. turned stay-at-home mom and wife, Cheryl delights in the stolen moments God gives her to write action- and faith-driven romance. She stays active in her church and in her laundry room. She's convinced that having been born on a naval base on Valentine's Day destined her to write military romance. A native of San Diego, California, Cheryl currently resides in beautiful, rustic southern Illinois, but has also enjoyed living in New Mexico and Oklahoma. Cheryl loves hearing from readers. You are invited to contact her at Cheryl@CherylWyatt.com or P.O. Box 2955, Carbondale, IL 62902-2955. Visit her on the Web at www.CherylWyatt.com and sign up for her newsletter if you'd like updates on new releases, events and other fun stuff. Hang out with her in the blogosphere at www.Scrollsquirrel.blogspot.com or on the message boards at www.SteepleHill.com.

Steadfast Soldier
Cheryl Wyatt

Steeple
Hill®

Published by Steeple Hill Books™

STEEPLE HILL BOOKS

Steeple Hill®

Recycling programs for this product may not exist in your area.

ISBN-13: 978-0-373-81483-1

STEADFAST SOLDIER

www.SteepleHill.com

Printed in U.S.A.

My heart, O God, is steadfast, my heart is steadfast;
I will sing and make music.

—*Psalms* 57:7

Dear Jesus, thank You for being a fisher of men. Love You, Lord. To Mom and Dad, who raised me to know I'm worth something in your eyes and God's. I'm blessed to have you. I appreciate you teaching me and Lisa to bait our hooks and cast our own lines, even when one goes astray. Sorry, Dad! You wanted your ear pierced, right? Grin. To Rachel Z at Books & Such for your friendship, industry insight and career guidance. To Melissa Endlich and Sarah McDaniel for loving these characters and believing in my books.

Acknowledgments

Thanks to this book's research helpers:

—Kim and Jeremy Woodhouse for your gracious insight into things boat-related. May all your bass be over ten pounds!

—Mary and Ivan Connealy also for help with fishing-boat stuff. Ivan, don't believe a word Mary tells you about those silly Seeker-villains. Snicker.

—Kim Lunato and Janet Klein for occupational and speech therapy research help, and Cara Putman for introducing me to these contacts.

—Animal therapy expert Eric Gillaspy and Megan DiMaria for this research contact.

—Tina Radcliffe for sharing the inspirational animal-rescue video.

—Janna Ryan for coming up with Chloe's name. Thanks!

Chapter One

"Talk about unconventional." U.S. Air Force pararescue jumper Chance Garrison shoved the gauzy curtain away from the glass pane cooled by the overworked air conditioner. He blinked to make sure his eyes weren't playing tricks on him as he stared at what was coming up the yard he'd just mown.

He pivoted to face his teammate and best bud, Brock, who approached where he stood near the window.

"What?" Brock joined him and tracked his gaze.

"Maybe that's not her." Chance pulled his sweat-dampened shirt away from his chest and leaned in. Yep. The woman—and the hairy *thing* dragging her—were definitely headed up the long driveway of the house Chance had rented for himself and his dad, who was recovering from a stroke he suffered following the death of Chance's mom. "What kinda person brings her pet to work?"

Brock pressed his face against the window. "A

cute one." He shouldered himself closer and elbowed Chance out of the way, presumably to get a better look. "*Very* cute."

Chance had noticed that too. But the fact that the pretty, young occupational therapist was lugging toward them the biggest, blackest Labrador retriever he'd ever seen was taking his attention away from how cute she was.

For the moment.

"Surely she's not thinking of bringing that animal in here." Brock tracked the odd pair's approach.

"She c-can't. If Dad sees that th-thing in the house, his blood pressure w-w-will hit the roof." Chance scowled at the stutter and eyed the bedroom door where Dad had retreated to watch midday game shows.

The TV blared through the thick walls, which meant Dad probably didn't have his hearing aid in.

When the woman stepped onto the landing with *dogzilla* rather than secure him to the lamppost, Chance's faith that Dad would comply with his new therapist and his regimen of home therapy drained, as if someone pulled the plug on the only hope left somewhere inside him, like a bathtub quickly draining.

But his teammates' wives trusted this woman, and he trusted his teammates' wives. If they crooned that this unconventional therapist could make a difference with Dad, he'd give it a shot. But what was the deal with the dog?

Regardless, he'd see to it that the animal stayed outside.

Chance opened the door and was greeted with the satisfying smell of fresh-cut grass and a smile on the therapist's face that was so radiant his concentration fled. So did his resolve to order the dog to stay outside. The sudden pounding in his chest when this woman held his gaze and flashed her brilliant smile wasn't something he'd been remotely prepared for.

Nor was he prepared for the luxurious sheen of her brown-gold hair or the vibrance of her eyes. The green of them matched the glistening beads in her diamond-shaped earrings, dangling beside beautifully sloped cheeks. As he looked closer, he realized that the little circles in the earrings were tiny onyx paws.

Before he knew what he was doing, Chance's hand inched toward them. Then Brock bumped his arm, and Chance realized he was staring. He dropped his hand quickly and dipped his chin to find blades of grass clinging to his rather ripe T-shirt. At least his deodorant was pulling double duty. Hopefully.

Chance raised his gaze back to her.

The woman's grin extended, and her generous lips parted to reveal shiny, silver braces. Her easy gaze slid to Brock for the slightest moment, then returned readily to Chance. And stayed.

Shyness swooped in like a stealth bomber, even as ripples of delight over the prolonged eye contact tried to intercept it.

"Hi," Chance managed. He concentrated on not stumbling over Brock's jump boots as he stepped back to let her in.

Smiling, Brock nodded a greeting to the therapist, then moved toward the bedroom. "I'll help your dad into his transfer chair."

"Hi," the therapist replied to Chance and stepped fully inside the door. With dogzilla. She extended her hand. "You must be Chance. I'm Chloe."

"Miss C-C-Callett." Chance engulfed her petite hand in his and gave it a polite shake. Quiet confidence returning, he directed a not-so-polite nod to the dog. "Uh, not sure how to s-say this, but Dad doesn't particularly care for animals in the house."

Chloe knelt, patting the beast. "That's all right. He's not really an animal. This is Midnight, my assistant."

Assistant? An unintended laugh tumbled from Chance's mouth. "A *dog is your assistant?*"

She rose, braced smile stiffening. "Yes. My specialty is that I use rescued animals to help rehabilitate humans."

Instant remorse hit Chance with a thud. "Look, I didn't m-mean to offend...." He stepped closer to Chloe and her mutt, who actually was kind of cute. Though not as cute as the girl.

Chance cleared his throat and was trying to formulate a more articulate apology when Chloe graced him with another stunning smile, this one as genuine as the first. "It's okay, really. I get that reaction a lot."

She gave the dog a command and he stood. "I know this is a shock if you're not used to it, but please, for your father's sake, trust us?"

"Us?"

"Us." She placed an affectionate, protective palm on Midnight's massive head. The deep compassion he detected in her voice when she spoke of his dad helped Chance nod without hesitation. The sincerity in her expression and tone enveloped him in familiar warmth.

"Your eyes remind me of my late mother's hugs."

Yikes! No idea what made him blurt that. Stress maybe.

Chloe paused, blinked. "Thanks." She passed Chance and smiled again. Her very essence enchanted him. The perfume, vivid makeup, neon-green nail polish, shiny lime patent-leather sandals and colorful geometric sundress didn't hurt.

If he could sum up Miss Callett in one word, it would be *alive*. Full of life and loving it.

He hoped some of that would rub off on his dad.

"M-may I offer you something to d-d-drink, Miss Callett?"

"Nope. I'm good." She grinned. "And it's Chloe."

He smiled. Mostly because he'd run out of anything to say. Chloe eyed the living room, which made Chance wish he'd cleaned up evidence of all the fast food and takeout he'd been ordering lately.

"With moving and work and taking care of Dad plus getting a house ready to sell, I don't have time to cook." Chance felt like he needed to explain.

He wrestled a pile of foam containers from the coffee table and dumped them in a trash bag. "Life at this point consists of convenience, which means less h-h-home-cooked and lots of takeout."

"Understandable. Does Ivan like home-cooked meals?"

"Yeah, but I'm not that great of a cook and he's picky." Thankfully, his dad's appetite was still healthy, unlike Chance's, which had atrophied a lot, like his father's now-unused hands.

A thoughtful look entered her captivating eyes. "I noticed from Ivan's medical history that he doesn't have dietary restrictions other than sodium. Do you?"

"No, ma'am."

"What does he like to eat?"

Where was she going with this? "Old-fashioned meat and potatoes."

"And you?"

"That suits me too." They both liked lots of red meat, even though it supposedly clogged the pipes. Chance hadn't been eating or sleeping well for months, and it was definitely starting to take its toll.

"That's good. Protein to feed your muscles for all that bodybuilding I can tell you do." She winked, causing his cheeks to flush. He brought his hand up to feel the scorch.

"Do you compete?" She pulled items from her bag.

"No, ma'am. I have to stay in this kind of shape for my job." That elicited her attention, and the respect he saw in her gaze suddenly added an extra benefit to all the daily pain and strain he put in at his team leader Joel's gym. Chance instantly felt ten feet taller and two tons of stress lighter.

"I see." Chloe pivoted in a graceful circle and eyed the room. "Are either of you allergic to flowers?"

What did flowers have to do with anything? he wondered, but just said, "No."

Lifting her pixie chin, Chloe appeared quite pleased with herself; her grin looked to harbor a well-planned secret. Her eyes veered toward his stack of Bible study books. Curiosity flitted across her features until her vision snagged on one book... then soured.

Why?

He eyed the title, *Becoming an Effective Youth Pastor.* He returned his gaze to her.

Professional mask back in place, she folded petite hands in front of her trim middle. "Shall we get started?"

Chance nodded concession to her as she stepped boldly toward the ruckus forming at his dad's bedroom door.

"I don't need anyone coming in here and telling me what to do!" Ivan could be heard loud and clear.

Chance cringed. Dad's mood was already festering, and he was about to see a dinosaur of a dog. In the house.

"And what in tarnation is *that?*" Ivan now squinted at his first glimpse of the massive black dog. He yanked his glasses from his chest pocket, squinted even more, and jabbed his good finger at Midnight. "Who let that heap-a-hair in here?" he bellowed and scowled at Chance.

Before Chance could offer an explanation, Chloe stepped forward. "Hi, Mister Garrison. I'm Chloe Callett. This is Midnight. We're here to assess your need for in-home OT, better known as occupational therapy."

"We? What's that doggone mutt got to do with it?" Ivan glowered at Chloe to the point that drool fell from the weak side of his sullen mouth.

Brock dabbed it with a red, bandit-style kerchief hanging loosely around Ivan's neck. Ivan let him but grunted. Brock pretended not to notice. He tried to finish discreetly until Ivan skewered him with a glare.

"On that note, I'll let myself out. Good luck," he said to Chloe and Chance and chuckled his way out the door.

Chloe didn't cringe at Brock's rapid departure or cower under Ivan's escalating disapproval and hollers, even though his pinched face shaded redder by the second.

Ivan's bulging eyes wrinkled at the corners and his nose squished up as he went nose to nose with Chloe. "What have you got stuck in your teeth there?"

"Braces."

"Aren't you too old for that?"

She shrugged and bit back a grin. "Maybe."

Ivan scowled. "Ask me, it's a waste of good money. My boy there's got crooked teeth and he's not bothered by it."

He wasn't?

True. He wasn't.

Until Chloe's gaze fell on his mouth. His face heated again. "*Au contraire,* Dad. I h-have one tooth that doesn't s-sit right. One." Chance chuckled and held up a pointer finger.

He also placed a clandestine hand on Ivan's shoulder and prepared to squeeze if his manners bounced any further out of bounds. The stroke had definitely adversely affected his father's cognitive and social judgment. Chance didn't mind his dad taking pokes at him, but Ivan was picking on Chloe. Chance would intervene. "Dad, we have a lady present."

As Chance increased pressure of his hand, Ivan stared Chance down, then swerved his head back toward Chloe. "Say, how old are you anyway? You married? 'Cause my son here is not, and it's about time he took the plunge."

Chance clamped his mouth shut and his hand tighter and tried not to laugh at the shocked look on Chloe's face. He cast an apologetic glance her way while his dad prattled on.

Undaunted other than a slight flush to her cheeks, Chloe calmly pulled a clipboard out and knelt in front of Ivan's chair. She made a couple of adjustments on the footrest then reached for Ivan's hand. "Squeeze for me?"

Ivan scowled but squished her hand with his good one. Hard. Harder than Chance thought necessary.

Chloe grimaced but her eyes grinned. "Nice grip. You've got the hands of a hardworking man."

A sliver of a smile creased the unaffected side of Ivan's mouth. The scowl eased from his face and a twinkle dared to dance in his eyes.

Until Chloe reached for his affected hand. "Now let's try the other one."

Back came the scowl. "Don't you read anything in that chart? My stroke made it so I can't do the other one."

She smiled sweetly. "Try." She held his listless hand.

A grunt. More intent scowling. But no response from his hand.

"I know you don't like dogs in your house. So go ahead. Squeeze and pretend you're knocking me upside the noggin for bringing Midnight in here." She winked.

Ivan blinked as though surprised by her candor, then bit back what might have been either the beginnings of a smile or a taunt, Chance couldn't be certain which one.

Ivan's wrist strained in effort, but his fingers didn't move and his hand didn't clench. His countenance fell. "Told ya! It's no use. I'm a useless man." He looked away.

Pain streaked through Chance. He wanted to drop to his knees and beg: *Dad, don't give up. Please don't give up.*

Compassion filled Chloe's expression. "Try again, Ivan. Please."

"Why? Got nothing other'n Chance left to live for. And he'd do fine without me."

"I'm sure he doesn't want to have to do without you. So come on. Try." She held her hand out closer to Ivan. They stared at each other in a state of silent stalemate.

Then fury flashed over Ivan's face. He glared at

Chloe's outstretched hand and growled. Then he called her names that would have sent a weaker woman sobbing from the house. Jaw clenched, Chance pinched Ivan's shoulder to get the message across to be respectful to the lady. "Dad, that's quite enough." Chance felt mortified.

But Chloe, serene, didn't budge. After a moment, she knelt closer and whispered, "I think your late wife would want you to try. I know Chance does." Chloe winked. "Think of all the beautiful grandbabies you have to look forward to in the future. They'd want you to try."

At first, Ivan scowled again. But as her words finally seeped in, he blinked several times. Met Chance's gaze, which had been reduced to pleading. Ivan's face softened. With a quaky motion, Ivan brought his hand to hers. A clumsy tremor proved his attempt to squeeze with all his might.

"Not bad." Chloe made notes on her paper, then stood.

"So, what do you think?" Fear streaked through Chance that Chloe would turn them away as clients.

Then reassurance sparkled like the gold in Chloe's eyes as she met his gaze briefly before grinning at Ivan. "I think by the time Midnight and I get through with Ivan, he'll be strong enough to pick us both up and toss us in the yard. With his affected arm."

Relief rushed Chance at the confidence in her words.

Ivan sat straighter. "You saying the sooner I do my exercises, the sooner you and that oversize mutt'll go away and not bother me anymore?"

"That's what I'm saying." Chloe repositioned Ivan's hand on a small towel from her bag. She rolled it, then secured it with tape and rested it on the table beside Ivan. "Curl your fingers around this. Squeeze whenever you think about it."

"Only if I can think of pinching the nose off that mongrel pup so everybody'll quit controlling my life."

"Fair enough." Chloe said a command to the dog, who'd been sitting obediently, stoic and watching.

At her command, Midnight lay down. He also switched from watching Chloe to watching Ivan while Chloe performed more physical, neurological and strength tests.

Ivan peered over his age-thickened nose at the dog and muttered something Chance couldn't hear. Chloe looked like she might balk. Chance moved to intervene.

Subtly, Chloe shook her head at him. He paused.

His respect for her rose as he observed Chloe's skill and bedside manner, especially in the glaring light of his father's storm of stubbornness. She wasn't asking him to do the assessment maneuvers. Nor demanding. Just not really giving Ivan the option to opt out. Smart girl. She'd pegged his difficult dad and his needs in a heartbeat.

Chance grinned. Maybe he liked this OT and her unconventional ways more than he cared to admit.

But if Ivan forbade the dog, they were done. There'd be nothing left to do except give up. Chance couldn't do that. He eyed the Lab, now sleeping near

Ivan's feet. It'd take a miracle to get Dad to accept help from a supersize fur-ball that looked more like a small bull than a dog.

Chloe gathered her things and suggested a few exercises to Ivan that Chance doubted he'd do. The therapist smiled and started to say something to Chance until her vision again brushed past the books on the table. Her smile faded. "So which one of you is studying to be a pastor, you or Brock?"

Chance laughed. "Definitely not Brock."

"That means you." Not a question but a flat statement.

He nodded, observing her face as it seemed to harden a bit. She eyed her watch, bade them goodbye and headed for the door.

Thunder rumbled in the distance. He watched her rush toward her car in a near-sprint that communicated her sudden need to flee—and not just from the impending bad weather.

Her speed birthed a concern in Chance that she might not intend to return, even though she had seemed to allude to the fact that she would.

He raised his gaze from Chloe to the darkening sky above the streets of Refuge, the town that claimed to live up to its name. Hopefully, in Ivan's case, that'd be true because he hadn't been happy about leaving St. Louis.

Chance braced his hand against the window, fingertips brushing remnants of blue in a changing sky whose only light seemed to be fading. Chance's fingers stretched, reaching for the only bright spot left in what appeared to be an angry, brewing storm he felt was symbolic. Bright spots were few and far between these days, and storms were nothing new to Chance lately. His heart latched on to the one thing that had been his steadfast anchor in the worst waves.

Prayer.

His lifeline to the One who draped that sky above the earth like a protective dome that brought comfort in dark days. He'd been an avid skydiver before, but after the twin tragedies of losing Mom, followed quickly by Dad's stroke, Chance spent even more time in the air. It made him feel closer to God and further from losing his mind in the midst of grief— grief that was trying to ground his soaring career and nix his newfound faith.

Chloe's vivid style and expressive face traipsed across his mind. When the woman with the contagious smile and neon zest for life had entered his rental home, it'd been like the world had breathed a fresh breath of life back into the room.

"Lord, bring her back. And let her be running for shelter from the storm rather than fleeing from Dad's stubbornness. He needs her help more than he's capable of realizing right now. So do I, and I'm not too proud to admit it. Please don't let her be changing her mind."

Chapter Two

If she was in her right mind, she'd change it, Chloe thought.

Two things wouldn't let her: Compassion that had clutched her for this grief-stricken family. And the rays of hope lifting melancholy clouds from the younger man's staggeringly handsome face when she'd made slight progress with his grumpy, stubborn dad.

His very noncompliant, curmudgeonly dad.

Yep, this case would definitely be a stretch. "But we've broken tougher barriers and overcome worse, huh, boy?"

She hadn't intended to start seeing patients until she got her animal-assisted therapy program off the ground. But Mandy had asked for a favor, so she'd made an exception to do a free consult on Mr. Garrison. Mandy was the reason Chloe had received clearance to start a satellite clinic in Refuge, and she owed Mandy, a friend of the Garrisons.

After being at the Garrison home, Chloe couldn't turn her back on them. Not even for her program. After all, helping people was the reason she wanted the program in the first place. And clearly they needed help.

"Poor Ivan," Chloe said to Midnight, whose ears rose.

No doubt the loss of his wife of over forty years had sucked the wind out of the sails of Ivan's will to live. She recognized it because she'd seen it in her mother.

Chloe remembered when Mom fell into a grief-driven depression after Chloe's workaholic father died. Her workaholic *pastor* father.

The books on the Garrisons' coffee table came to mind, as did the revelation that they belonged to Chance.

Chloe didn't want to ponder why that thought plunked dots of disappointment into her tummy.

Chloe's father was an emotionally absent minister who'd left Chloe feeling like marriage would mean the end of her personal dreams, the way it had for her mother. Still, Chloe knew Mom had loved Dad and was devastated by his death. She had temporarily lost her will to live, but thankfully, Mom pulled out of it, thanks to God and animal therapy.

Once Ivan's will to live returned, it would be too late to rehabilitate. If Ivan was to regain any use of the limbs that stroke had affected, the time for therapy was now. Urgency in the son's striking eyes as he'd watched her work with his father proved he knew it too.

She wondered what Chance did for a living. He was so muscular that Chloe couldn't imagine what kind of job required that fierce of a commitment to stay physically fit. It was the kind of boulder-rugged build that a businesswoman like herself never saw in the suits she'd dated in Chicago. Plus, he was familiar with medical terms and had used some when they had talked on the phone to arrange her visit.

Not that she was thinking of dating Mr. Muscles or anything. She just liked to know who she was dealing with. Sure, that was it. Chloe fanned her face with Ivan's paperwork.

Though the overcast sky had dropped the temperature outside, the temperature inside the car rose a bit with each image of Chance that scrolled across the screen in her mind. It left her feeling befuddled and bereft and inexplicably unsettled.

Standing in the overpowering presence of an unbelievably good-looking guy should *not* make her feel like she'd stepped in the path of an oncoming tsunami. Not even if he was quite possibly the most amazingly gorgeous man she'd ever laid eyes on.

Speaking of storms, Chloe eyed the skies as she sat in her car with her medical charts and stared at the black clouds that had gathered above the Garrison home. Boxes had been strewn everywhere, proving the men had just moved in but hadn't gotten everything settled yet.

The despair vying for hope on the son's handsome face had yanked Chloe's heartstrings. She finished her medical charting and pulled away from the curb.

By the time Chloe navigated her SUV to the stop sign at the end of the long street, hail pelted her car and rain slapped the windshield. She twisted the knob. Wipers slashed across the relentless film of falling water.

She punched buttons on her GPS. "Okay, Miss G. Left or right?" Having only been in Refuge a few days, she was unfamiliar with the residential streets. Before arriving at the Garrison home, she'd come from a meeting with Mandy at Refuge's hospital, a different direction than her mom's home.

The arrow in the GPS screen pointed left, but despite her wipers running full speed ahead, visibility was poor.

The wind picked up, blowing sheets of rain sideways. Her SUV trembled in their power. She tried to peer out her side windows. Water rushed in rivulets, distorting her view. Midnight whined and moved closer to her.

"I know, boy. You're scared of storms." Chloe nibbled her lip and eyed the dark sky. Didn't they have bad storms here? Wasn't Refuge part of Tornado Alley? Her native Chicago was six hours north and the weather drastically different than in southern Illinois.

She peered in her rearview mirror long enough to consider returning to Chance's house for cover.

Normally she'd feel weird seeking shelter from a stranger. But something about Chance reminded her of home, and in a good way. He seemed the sort who would be like a protective big brother. Or the ideal best friend everyone wished they had. Strong and honest and stalwart. Yet loving and kind and hospitable. The slight drawl and sweet southern manners, endearingly shy demeanor, crooked smile and deep dimples didn't hurt either.

Chloe let out a long groan. She applied the brakes to her mind and pressed her foot to the gas of her SUV.

She'd rather contend with a potential twister than this attraction trying to twist up her insides.

Three blocks later, Chloe regretted her decision to weather the storm. No choice now but to drive through it. The wind howled outside and Midnight howled inside.

Slowing, she pressed a hand on his thick neck. "It's okay, boy. Shhh. You're fine, buddy."

Rain increased to the point that she couldn't see her hood, much less the road, wherever it was. White-knuckling the wheel, she pulled her car over to what she hoped was a curb and put on her hazard lights.

"I hope no one crashes into us, Midnight. Of course, I'm probably the only dummy out here trying to drive through what appears to be an inland hurricane."

Pounding at her window drew her attention and elicited a shriek she didn't realize slipped out of her until Midnight surged up and growled at the figure outside.

A very tall, broad figure that caused her heart to beat faster than the rain sloshing back and forth with her useless wipers.

Even through the darkened sky and thrashing rain, she'd recognize that crooked smile anywhere. Chance.

He stood with a sopping newspaper failing to shield his wet face. He moved his hand in a rapid circle. Trying to get her to roll her window down? She reached for her window button.

He shook his head and pointed to her passenger window. She unlocked the door. He rushed around, pulled the door open and slid like quicksilver into her seat, shoving the dog over in one smooth process. As roomy as her car's interior was, his massive frame filled it to capacity.

"Hey." Water trickled from his spiky military buzz. He dripped all over her just-cleaned seat. She didn't care.

She loosened her grip from the steering wheel. "Hey." *Handsome.* "I'm stuck."

He grinned. "I see that. Where are you trying to go?"

"My house."

He laughed. "And you don't know where it is?"

She giggled. "Actually, no, because it's my mom's house. I'm staying there while I'm here in Refuge."

His smile faded a shade. "Do you plan to leave soon?"

"I'd love to stay, but I have to get an animal-assisted therapy program off the ground in order to transfer my business from Chicago. I long to live in southern Illinois. Specifically here in Refuge, since my mom is here." Not only that, but also she was on a waiting list for her own place.

Chance stroked Midnight. "What brought her to Refuge?"

Chloe pondered how to answer. Chance was undoubtedly only asking to be polite. But just in case his interest was any deeper than that, she'd best tell him the truth.

"She wanted to move as far away as possible from my dad's mistress."

His jaw slackened and his face tilted. "Oh, wow. Sorry, Chloe. It was rude of me to pry."

"Doesn't matter." She sighed and scraped her fingernails along the rubber holding the glass in and realized two things: One, it felt purging to talk in the rain. Two, she liked his company and didn't want to leave it.

Chance shifted, but not because he seemed uncomfortable. He looked relaxed as he watched her. "I get the feeling you don't mind talking about it. Need to, maybe."

She shrugged. "I don't know. You just seem the type to be a good listener. Someone who'd understand."

Chance unlatched his seat belt and nodded. "I try. So, is your dad still with the mistress?"

Chloe couldn't help it; a laugh scraped out. "No. My dad's dead. He died when I was younger."

Chance shifted again. "Sorry, Chloe. That's rough."

"Yeah, well, just so you know, the mistress…was his church. He was a pastor who knew and cared for his congregation better than his wife or daughter."

She reached for the door handle. Not sure why. She'd said too much.

But Chance didn't flinch. He just leaned across and put his hand over hers to stop her departure. Then he grinned.

"What?" Of course, just where did she think she'd go in the rain? Ugh! His Handsomeness had the common sense section of her brain twisted like a bread twist tie.

"I was thinking about your caustic expression when you saw the books on my table. Now I know why." He smiled gently.

She laughed. "I guess I overreacted. But now you know I have an aversion to preachers of any sort."

His face cringed. "Wow, that doesn't bode well for me then." He leaned against his seat and pulled his arm back to his body, pausing midway to pinch her shoulder in a friendly, innocent nip. "We'd love to have you in Refuge. It would be good for you and your mom. So where does she live?" Rain pellets drove themselves into the windshield, surrounding them with pounding white noise. Chloe suddenly felt uncomfortable at the thought of how much she'd shared so soon with a virtual stranger.

Yet Chance didn't feel like one. He felt familiar. Like they were meant to meet and be friends.

"The street doesn't show up on there," she said when Chance eyed her GPS.

"Most in Refuge don't. That's partly because there's an unmapped military base nearby. Plus, Refuge is a small town. What's the address?"

"Two-twelve Haven Street."

His face lit. "That's down the street from my buddy's house. Manny and his wife, Celia. They live on Haven. Well, follow me." He jumped from her SUV and ran back to his vehicle.

Chance had hardly said ten words to her when she had visited his dad. But she'd just caught a glimpse of Chance unguarded.

"And, buddy, unfortunately I like what I see a tad too much. Keep me in line, okay?" Chloe told Midnight as the dog nudged her hand with his nose, then yelped when thunder rumbled. The dog was terrified of lightning too. She needed to get him inside or he'd end up in her lap and impede her windshield view.

Chloe pulled away from the curb as Chance passed her. Thankfully, he drove slowly. His brake lights became Chloe's compass. They beamed through the storm like two tiny red lighthouses. She followed his taillights in full trust.

Eventually Mom's house came into view. Chloe pulled into the driveway and waved Chance on, signaling he could go. Surely a man like that had somewhere important to be. She hated to detain him; he'd been so kind to get her home.

But he parked his Jeep and rushed from it toward her…with a parachute-shaped umbrella!

She opened her door. "Oh, Chance, you're getting drenched! Why didn't you pull that umbrella out before?"

"Because you were in the car before."

How sweet! "This isn't necess—"

But his adorably crooked grin melted the end of her sentence. She grabbed Midnight's leash and tried to lead him from the car.

He wouldn't budge. "Come on, boy!"

Chance held the umbrella over her and became totally soaked.

"What's wrong with him?" He nodded to the dog. Concern crossed Chance's face as Midnight's whines and trembling escalated.

"He has a serious phobia of storms. He normally leaps in my lap at the first clap of thunder or flash of lightning." Chloe tugged on the leash but Midnight eyed the formidable sky, then flopped to his belly in the seat.

The dog wasn't going anywhere unless someone made him.

"Here." Chance handed Chloe the umbrella and ran to the other side of the car. Opening the door, he reached in and—just lifted the dog. Not only that, he lifted the terrified monstrosity of a mutt as if he were a stuffed toy. Chance expertly carried him toward the house.

Midnight must have felt secure because he didn't struggle except to search for Chloe over Chance's well-developed shoulders and back.

Rain soaked his shirt and caused it to cling to his skin so every cut, corded muscle became visible as he sprinted with her dog to Mom's door.

She regretfully ripped away her gaze and rushed behind them with the unique umbrella.

Chloe's mom flung the door open. "What in the world?" Mary stepped aside as the dripping three-some filed in.

Chance stopped on the rug and set the dog down. "Midnight, stay," he said to the dog, which not only complied but eyed Chance like he was his new best friend.

"Good boy." Chance scrubbed Midnight behind his ears, then tipped his head at her mom. "Ma'am."

Mary ogled him. Chloe knew the feeling. Not often did one meet a guy who proved that chivalry was not dead, especially one so tall, broad and beautifully sculpted.

Chloe fiddled with her oversize wristwatch. "This is my mom, Mary. She is working for Mandy part-time as a receptionist in her doctor's office until she can get her greenhouse business up and running here."

"What do you grow?" Chance patted Midnight.

"Flowers, mostly." Mary snapped out of her gawking. "Oh, forgive my manners. Let's get you a towel and something to drink, young man."

"Thank you, but I'm fine. I need to get going." Chance shifted from foot to foot. "It was nice to meet you. Have a nice day, Mary."

He turned to Chloe. "Later." He slid her a lopsided grin, then slipped out the door and into the rain, leaving her speechless for the second time in her life.

Later. Sounded like a promise, as did the lazy way the word had drawled across his tongue. Despite rain-soaked clothes, Chloe broke out in a sweat.

"My goodness, but he's a looker!" Mary scuttled around the room.

Chloe's sentiments exactly. "He's a Good Samaritan on top of all those piles of muscles and mile-long legs."

"A strapping Samaritan. With no identifier that he's spoken for."

"I noticed that too," Chloe said in a small voice. Ringless finger. She didn't like that her eyes and heart had headed so quickly in that direction.

"Later. That sounded a little like an invitation. At the very least, an inquiry." Mary hawk-eyed Chloe.

Later. The softly spoken word and the part question, part promise in his silky-suave voice wilted her. For when the word had slid like sugar from Chance's handsome lips, she'd felt a surge of hope.

And hoping to see Chance again on a personal level was the absolute *last* thing she should be doing.

Especially if the man planned to be a pastor.

Mom returned with dry towels. "So who was that?"

Chloe draped one over herself then Midnight. "The son of the client I met with today. I couldn't find my way in the storm. He passed by and saw me. Helped me get here."

"And carried your wet, stinky dog in and gave you his umbrella and went without?" Mary drifted to the door as if to glimpse another look at the man who'd so thoroughly rescued her daughter.

"Yes, he is quite mannerly." Chloe curled her fingers around the umbrella and tried to ignore the compelling fragrance of Chance's cologne lingering on it.

Mary handed Chloe a piece of paper. "Evie of Refuge B&B phoned today. She has vacancies now."

Chloe took the message. "Oh, good. Thanks."

"You could stay with me a while longer."

"I know. But by setting down roots, the folks on my Chicago team will know I'm serious about presiding over the Refuge clinic if I get it going."

"When, not if."

Chloe reached over and kissed her mom's cheek. "That's what I love about you. Always believing in me." Chloe called Evie back then turned to her mom when she hung up the phone. "She has three newly remodeled, furnished rooms available at reasonable rent. She said to come on over."

"Want me to drive with you?" Mary asked.

"Nah. Stay out of the rain. Give your arthritis a rest. Evie said she has three keys, a box of dog biscuits and a pan of Mountain Dew Apple Dumplings ready and for me and Midnight to choose our favorite room."

Mary chuckled and walked Chloe to the door. "Sounds like Evie. Welcome to Refuge, Chloe."

If she could stay.

Chloe hadn't inherited all of Mom's optimism.

Chapter Three

"This one's my favorite." Chloe pulled out her neon-green therapy band at Ivan's next OT session.

Ivan's scowl intensified. "Who cares?"

"I do." Chance knelt. "Come on, Dad. Please try it."

"I said no. I'm tired of everyone bossing me around."

"We're trying to help you get better." Chance looked to Chloe. Desperation gnawed at him. Dad had refused therapy several days in a row. How long would she keep coming if Ivan refused to try?

"I'm sure Miss Callett has other places to be, Dad. She's been here three hours today already. Please, don't waste the lady's time."

Chloe put her hand on Chance's arm. "It's okay. We'll give it a rest for now." She rose and rolled up her band.

A sinking sensation hit Chance when she stuffed it, along with her clipboard, inside her bag.

Clearly she was done.

Ivan lifted his head. Eyed her and Chance, then turned away when they caught him looking.

"Thanks for trying." Chance walked Chloe to the door.

"No problem." But the sudden panic piercing her face when she eyed her watch belied her confident words. Chloe faced Chance. "I'm sorry I can't stay longer today. I've a meeting I'm late for. Bye, Chance."

She ran to her car. Midnight wasn't with her today. Chance appreciated that she'd tried without him.

Hadn't made a difference. He closed the door and fought his frustration with Dad.

"Next time you mow that yard, boy, mow this carpet too." Ivan tried to wheel himself across the floor, but the carpet was too thick and the chair wouldn't budge.

"Where do you need to go, Dad?"

"Anywhere you aren't. Put me to bed."

Chance clenched his jaw and pushed the chair across the floor to Ivan's room. "Dad—"

"Just let it go, son! Let me go. Just…let me go."

Chance's throat clogged. His eyes stung. "I can't." He helped his dad into bed and was surprised to see tears drip on his hands. His or Dad's? It didn't matter. They mingled. Chance tucked Ivan in. His father turned away. Glared at the wall.

"I know this is hard for you. I love you, Dad. Too much to let you go." His voice cracked.

A grunt met his words. But that was okay. Losing

Mom had ripped any reticence out of Chance about telling those he loved how he felt. His father just switched on the television and turned it up. The two men sat in silence, staring at the screen.

Two hours later, Chance heard a distinct rumble outside as a motorcycle pulled up. "Dad, Vince is here to visit with you while I make a grocery run." Chance stared at the figure in the bed. "Want anything special?"

"Yeah," his dad grunted a reply. "Celery, peanut butter and a roll of duct tape the width of your lips."

Chance grinned with relief. "For my mouth, right?"

"Yes, and a lock to keep that hippie therapist and her creature out of this prison you're forcing me to live in."

Chance chuckled grimly. "I'll think about it." He went to step out and close the door.

Ivan twisted. "Wait, what's wrong with the mutt?"

"Nothing that I'm aware of."

"Just wondered, since he was a no-show today."

Chance paused. Was it possible? Did his father actually care a little bit about Midnight?

Maybe there was hope after all. At this point, he'd grasp that tiny grain. His father's voice interrupted his thoughts.

"Get going. I need my nap. Don't forget celery. The one with hearts."

"The packages with the hearts are my favorite too," a voice that sounded like honey to his ears said behind him a few minutes later as he was eyeing the produce at the grocery store.

Chance turned. The smile was as sweet as the sound. "Hi, Chloe." He eyed her cart. "Shopping, I see?"

"Yes. Looks like you're stocking up too." She watched him set two packages of celery hearts in his cart as she rolled hers beside his.

"How's Ivan?" she asked.

"Calm for now." He grinned. "But only because he's sleeping."

She laughed. It swirled through him like fresh air.

"Thanks for being patient with him. I know you're going above and beyond what anyone else would do."

She put fresh broccoli in her cart. "It's what I'd want if he were my dad. I try to treat every patient as though they are people I love."

Chance paused. "I got the feeling you didn't care much for your dad."

Chloe stilled and twisted a knot in the broccoli bag. "He didn't care much for me. But I loved him. He was the only dad I had, and while he wasn't perfect, he was mine." She blinked several times.

Chance rested a hand on her arm. "Wanna go somewhere and hang out? We can just talk and have fun. I can show you around Refuge."

"I'd like that." She eyed her cart's contents. "I'll drop my stuff off at home and meet you back at your house?"

Chance nodded and a sense of excitement filled

him as he checked out and drove home. It lingered as he put groceries away.

Vince stepped out of Ivan's room. "I helped him bathe. He'll be in bed for the rest of the day and all night, I think. If you want to get out of the house for a bit, bro, I can sit with him. Val's preparing a court case. Trial's in two days, so she's working at home."

"Actually, I was going to ask if you could. I'm showing Dad's OT around Refuge."

Vince got a goofy smirk. "Sounds like a date."

"No, just a…a…friendship outing. I'm trying to stay in her good graces so she'll keep coming back to help Dad. Not sure why she hasn't given up on him yet." Chance swallowed and eyed his dad's door. A car pulled up outside. "That's her."

Vince grinned. "Have fun, man. You need it."

Outside, Chance walked Chloe to his Jeep. He opened the door and helped her up, pleased to discover she'd freshened up her makeup, clipped her hair into a barrette and spritzed on perfume.

"Where to first?" she asked as he drove toward Haven Street.

"Mandy mentioned you're looking for land to build your animal-assisted therapy program."

"Yeah, if it ever gets off the ground." She sighed.

"Having trouble?"

"That's an understatement. My troubles have trouble where the program's concerned. My meetings with Refuge City Council and the bank loan officer didn't go well today."

Remorse smacked him upside the heart. "Oh, wow.

That's where you were headed when you left late today."

"Yeah, but it wouldn't have mattered. Two council members are afraid of funding something so progressive."

"I think I know the two in question. Sheriff Steele and Mayor Bunyan?"

"Exactly. How'd you know?"

"Because they staunchly opposed programs my buddies and I tried to institute."

"I hope everything turned out well for you."

"We compromised. Steele and Bunyan agreed to what they did only because the entire town put pressure on them."

"That's discouraging. The town doesn't know me."

"But God does. If you have Him in your corner, there's no need to fear. Besides, the mayor and the sheriff are both entering their last terms."

Chloe laughed. "Not soon enough to save my program."

"Let me know if there's anything I can do to help."

"You believe in me?"

"Of course. You haven't given up on Dad yet."

Chloe nodded, seeing the fear in his eyes that she might. But as willing as she was to keep trying, she couldn't force Ivan to exercise. "You haven't either. So between the two of us and Midnight, he still has a chance."

"Thanks, Chloe. You encourage me."

"We're even then, because you encourage me too."

Chance took her to his friend Joel's house and

borrowed his four-wheeler. He rode Chloe through the woods until dense forest gave way to a clearing.

Chance cut the engine. Chloe liked being close to him and didn't want to put distance between them, but the view before them called to something deep in her. Almost like a dream.

"Wow." Chloe climbed off the ATV. "This land is incredible. I can instantly envision where each of our animal rescue buildings should go. Mallory, my cousin and partner in crime with the animal-assisted therapy project, would freak if she saw this."

Chance rested his hands on Chloe's shoulders and turned her to the left as he pointed at a real estate sign.

"It's for sale," Chloe breathed. She eyed every inch of the property and practically drooled. "This would be perfect." She turned to Chance. "Do you know who owns it?"

"The local garage owner. He has money coming out his ears. He owns a lot of land around Refuge. He'd probably sell it at a reasonable price as long as he knows the program is worthwhile."

"My program will bring job openings to Refuge."

"That'll help."

"But it may not be enough. There are too many obstacles to count."

"Think of them as hurdles. Just focus on the one directly in front of you. Leap one at a time."

"Thanks, Chance. Did you ever coach sports? You should."

"I ran track in high school and college, then

coached troubled teens in my spare time. I started a cross-country running club to try and give them something to do besides get arrested on weekends."

"So you have it in your heart to work with youth?"

"Yeah. It's very important to me."

She rubbed the chill off her arms and hoped he'd change the subject. He stilled and studied her motions a moment before leading her to the edge of the property. A stream gurgled beside grassy knolls. Breath left her body in a delicate gasp. He smiled gently at her.

"This is so peaceful, so picturesque." She turned in a half circle, then stopped. "That sign on the adjacent property says Sold. Do you know what's going in there?"

"One of my skydiving buddies bought it. He wants to put in a horse farm and bring at-risk teens out to teach them work ethic. He wants to use rescued horses, which is why I brought you here. If you snagged the property next door, you two could combine your programs."

"That would save money, which is another hurdle I need to jump in order to get this thing off the ground."

"I have no doubt. I believe you will."

She faced him. "I'm glad someone does. Let's hope you're not the only one in town."

The wind rustled tendrils of hair loose from her barrette. He visually tracked the motion as it billowed. Something melted in her.

Something that made the moment much too romantic.

His eyes met hers, then fell to the lush, green earth. He dug the tip of his boot into the ground. His countenance succumbed to shyness.

"Hey, that looks like a combat boot. Is it?" She nodded toward his foot.

He nodded. "Jump boot. Similar, I guess."

"For skydiving?"

He met her gaze again. "You could say that."

What he said intrigued her, but what he didn't say intrigued her more. She loved a man immersed in mystery. The fact that she'd get to ride back through forest and fields with her arms wrapped around him again pasted a smile on her face.

He looked so masculine against bright backdrops of raised knolls carpeted in vivid green grass landscaped with outlying woods. Assorted trees and wildflowers dotted the canvas of earth, which met the sky in brilliant purple-pink hues. Colorful and vibrant, pure and peaceful.

How she felt inside just walking and talking with him.

His jaw lifted as he eyed the painted horizon. "Sun's setting. We better head back."

Walking side by side, he peered down at her with steadfast sureness. The compelling look on his face caused her heart to flutter like a butterfly being courted by a winsome breeze.

"It's going to be okay, Chloe," he said after a moment of walking, with no words other than what was communicated by his sturdy gaze whispering unwavering confidence into hers.

"I hope so."

He cleared his throat. "Uh, d-do you think you'll be coming back t-t-to try again, y-you know, w-w-with Dad?" He looked both annoyed at his stutter and scared of her answer. His dysfluent speech proved it so.

She stopped, put her hand on his arm until he paused his long-legged stride and looked down at her. "Of course."

He nodded and relief fell across his face in terrific waves. He resumed his steps. The four-wheeler came into view. "Busy week ahead."

"Me too." One that she looked forward to more than she ought, thanks to thoughts of glimpsing Chance again, although she truly did look forward to the challenge of assisting Ivan with his exercises.

If she could continue to trick or otherwise convince him to do them. If not, Chance had no need of her. She was there to help his father and she'd best not forget it.

That's the only reason Chance looked at her as if he'd been stranded for months in the middle of a lonely, swirling ocean and she was the first lifeline to hit his destitute horizon. Right?

God had sent her. No doubt about it. The girl was a human life preserver. Dad's mood had improved three hundredfold since Midnight and Chloe had come this week. And his mood had improved along with his dad's, especially after spending time with her yesterday afternoon and evening. They'd had a great time.

Chance's teammate Nolan and his wife, Mandy, arrived, and Chance grabbed his keys. "Mandy's here, Dad. She's gonna sit with you while Nolan and I work out and run by the Drop Zone. See you later, Dad."

Ivan waved him off. Apparently, Dad's mood still had a ways to go.

After pausing in the driveway to catch Mandy up on his dad's needs, Chance and Nolan left. They pulled up at the B&B to pick up Brock for their daily pararescue workout regimen at Joel's.

Hopefully the next few hours of strenuous lifting and exhausting himself on free weights, kettlebell and fitness machines that looked more like torture devices would sweat the image of Chloe, the memory of her essence and the linger of her perfume out of Chance's mind.

Joel had built an exercise pole barn on his property. The guys used it often to stay in the superior shape their jobs required. If Chance's appetite would return and his insomnia go, he'd be up to par. But these days, eating felt like little more than cramming gritty rocks in his mouth.

After cardio and working muscles to the max, they hit the gym showers and locked up. Brock dropped Nolan off at the Drop Zone to help Joel, then accompanied Chance to the car.

"Good ol' Thursday. One more work day. We going out this weekend?" Brock pulled out of the DZ driveway.

Chance knew that by *weekend,* Brock meant

Friday night, since Saturday evenings the guys convened at Joel's or Commander Petrowski's for PJ cookouts.

Chance attended church on Sundays now and didn't want to break away from Dad or find sitters on Saturdays to attend the PJ barbecues, though he missed them. Dad was anxious about being left alone, plus his doctor recommended he remain under constant watch for a few more weeks.

"What's popping at the movies?" Chance settled deeper into the seat of Brock's sports car and enjoyed the rumble of power beneath him. Brock was as much of an adrenaline junkie as Chance. They hadn't gotten to do much in the way of fun the past six months though.

Merging onto the interstate, Brock rocked the RPMs. "I'll check the movie schedule at home. There's a new action flick on."

Since Chance had openly committed his life to Christ following his teammate Vince's dramatic conversion, Brock didn't pressure Chance to party. Chance hadn't managed to talk Brock into attending Bible studies…yet. In due time.

Brock changed lanes and passed a semi. "You could invite that girl."

Chance plucked a bag of Nutter Butters off the dash. He had a penchant for sweets and missed his mom's baking. These would get him through. "What girl?"

"You know what girl." Brock grinned. "She's new to town. You should make her feel welcome."

A jagged piece of cookie must have gone down wrong, as Chance coughed. "The dog-toting OT?"

"Seriously, man. She could probably use friends."

Brock was right. Mandy told him in the driveway earlier she was the only person Chloe knew in Refuge besides her mom. And now Chance and his father.

Chance worked kinks out of his shoulder. "Not to change the subject, but I need to get back into a better routine. I don't want to be out of shape for a rescue."

"Long as you keep working out like a fiend and hit most of the training ops, you'll be fine."

"But being youngest on the team, I'm the weak link."

"You're more experienced than most guys on Petrowski's other PJ teams. Dude, seriously, don't sweat it. You've been through a lot. Take this time to regroup."

Chance flipped the visor up when Brock merged onto Pena's Landing toward the B&B. "I just wanna keep my head in the game when lives are at stake. Ya know?"

"For sure." Brock pulled into the driveway, cut the ignition and leaned forward abruptly. "No way."

Chance looked up. Blinked. Leaned in. "Is that Chloe?" She sat on the B&B steps, looking uncharacteristically frustrated. Chance exited the car. Brock trailed.

Chloe's body tensed and her expression looked uncertain under the wraparound porch's dim light until she recognized the guys. She rose and wiped grime off of jeans that outlined shapely legs. "Hey."

They stopped in front of her at the foot of the stairs. When she looked at Chance as if she could cry on his shoulder, his heart melted. "Hey, Chloe. What's up?"

She waved a hand up to the tree where soft mewling originated. "There's a stray kitten loose. I didn't know it and Midnight got after him. He's stuck up there. I'm not fond of falling from heights."

"I assume the dog's inside?"

She nodded. Chance searched the tree until he spotted the kitten's eyes glowing between still-wet leaves that clung to a tangle of branches.

"Can you help me rescue him?"

Her voice drew his attention back. "Rescue?"

He was falling for her right here on the spot.

This was a girl after his heart.

Brock clamped Chance's shoulder. "It just so happens that rescue is his specialty. Particularly animals and people." Brock headed inside.

Chloe's face fell, which meant she didn't realize Chance wouldn't need help getting the kitten safely down. "Brock has allergies. Cats and guinea pigs."

"Oh. I suppose you'll need my help?" She nibbled her lip, which unfortunately drew his gaze there and interrupted his focus. He struggled to decipher what she'd just said.

Thankfully, the recall that had earned him the PJ team job of memorizing intel didn't elude him long. "I think I can manage. But you can watch if you want." He grinned.

She stepped aside. "Okay. Do I need to do anything?"

"No, ma'am." Except answer the question burning tracks through his brain. "Other than clue me in on what you're doing here." It wasn't often he came home to a beautiful woman waiting at his door. Well, not *his* door. But still.

"I might ask you the same thing," she said, her typical spunk returning.

"I live here. Well, used to, with Brock."

She eyed the Victorian structure. "Oh. You did?"

"Yep. Miss Evie rented rooms to most of my team before they married their sweethearts."

"Your special rescue team?"

"Yeah, how'd you know I'm on a rescue team?"

Even the cover of moonlight couldn't camouflage the tinge invading her cheeks. "Um, er, Mandy might have mentioned it. I hope that was okay."

He nodded. Not many people knew the elite status their team held in the U.S. military. Chloe might not know he was an Air Force special operative, but by the obvious respect in her eyes, she knew plenty well he was highly trained, distinguished military.

"I was staying with Mom, but Evie had a vacancy."

"Need help moving your stuff in?"

"No, I didn't bring much from Chicago because I'm not sure how long I'll be staying. But thanks."

Silent, Chance went to his Jeep. "Let me get some rope and we'll get Miss Maple out of the tree."

Chloe followed in a skip. "Miss Maple?"

"Yeah. She got herself stuck like syrup up there in a maple tree, and she looks like a clump of wet leaves clinging to the branch. So Miss Maple fits."

She peered at the frightened kitten. "What if she's a he?"

"Then we'll call it Mr. Maple."

"We?" She rose on tiptoes.

"Correction. You. It's obviously a stray and Dad would cream my corn if I brought a cat in the house."

Her finger went up. "Hey, that could work."

"What?"

"Use the cat as a ploy to get your dad moving."

Chance laughed, knowing she was joking but having fun with the mental images her statement provoked nonetheless. "Yeah, that'd do it. Can you imagine? He'd bullet out of that chair after me faster than I could say *kitty litter*."

They both knew they were working against time in terms of Ivan regaining the use of his hands. But it felt good to see the rare humor in the situation.

She giggled, causing a carefree breeze to blow through him. He found himself slowing to allow her to fall into step beside him.

He also found himself laughing, genuinely laughing, for the first time in six long, hard months.

Chapter Four

Chloe felt fantastic when she heard Chance let loose and laugh like that. He caught her gaze and grinned.

"You look like a coon in a food-infested campground."

"It's the company." He winked at her. Slow and sweet and scrumptious.

She drank it in like sipping her favorite tea as they meandered together, steps in sync, to the maple tree.

He donned gloves, scaled the treacherous tree as though it were a simple stepladder and rescued the kitten, all in under seventeen seconds.

Joy fluttered through her as he let go of the lowest branch and landed squarely on the ground. Tenderness coated her insides like invisible honey, sweet and soothing, as he cradled the kitten protectively like a baby. He rubbed fingers lightly over it in calming motions.

His lopsided victory grin as he approached was a bonus treat. She stepped close, careful not to make a commotion. The baby kitty panted in wide-eyed wariness and wiggled deeper into Chance's embrace.

Seeing something that small and fragile nestled next to his sturdy bicep did something funny to her insides. Like supersonic melting.

She reached to pet the kitten.

It hissed until Chance rested a calming hand on its fuzzy head and murmured soothing words. The whisper went through the recesses of her soul. Places no one had access to. She started to step back, but he gathered the kitten into his protective palms and passed the tiny critter to her.

It leapt to make a getaway but calmed the instant Chance's hand blanketed its back. The kitten settled in her arms under his touch. Eyed him in adoring trust and mewed.

Chloe's heart bent toward him in much the same manner.

Careful, this one could trip your heart up and hinder every dream you have.

He tugged out a cell phone. "I have a friend looking for a pet." After conversing a few minutes, he ended the call and scratched the kitten under the chin until it purred. "Good news, little one. We found you a good home on the first try."

"They want the kitten?" Elation and thankfulness skittered through Chloe. God had quickly answered her prayers for the abandoned animal.

"Yep. They're on the way now. It's my buddy Ben Dillinger. His stepdaughter even likes the name we picked out." Chance walked with Chloe to the steps.

They sat hip to hip and petted the contented kitten until Chance's friends arrived.

"We'll take Miss Maple to Refuge's vet in the morning," Amelia, Ben's wife, assured Chloe, who offered them one of her pet carriers for the now-playful kitty.

Reece hugged Chloe and Chance. "Thank you! I love Miss Maple already. I promise to take good care of her."

"Reece wants to be a vet when she grows up," Ben, the tallest, cutest Asian-American man Chloe had ever seen, said as he brushed a fatherly hand along Reece's hair, which haloed her face in ringlets.

Chloe knelt. "You do? My cousin Mallory is training to be a vet. She's almost finished."

"Maybe she can come work in Refuge," Reece said as she hugged the kitten as it purred to the point that it vibrated.

Chance walked alongside Chloe as they accompanied the Dillinger family to their car with their new pet. "Refuge currently only has one vet. He's an older gentleman looking to retire. He's scaling severely back on business."

Which meant another wrench in Chloe's plans.

Amelia eyed Chloe carefully, as did Chance, observing as her steps stuttered and face fell.

"Thank you, Chloe, for caring about animals. I do hope you get to stay in Refuge." Amelia hugged her. "You really brighten Chance's days," she whispered before pulling away.

For some reason Amelia's caring statement lodged

in Chloe's throat, blocking words momentarily. "Thanks. Good to meet you. Miss Maple's in loving hands."

Chloe felt Chance's eyes on her as the Dillingers piled in the car with an excited Reece and the contented kitten. Ben's family waved as they pulled away.

Chance drew near. "You okay, Chloe?"

She sighed. "If I have no vet willing to come aboard, I have no foundation for an animal-assisted therapy program." Chilled, she rubbed her arms. He followed her motions, then removed his denim jacket and draped it around her shoulders. She didn't mind that he let his hands linger there a moment. "Thanks, Chance."

He wrapped a friendly arm around her shoulder and pulled her in for a quick hug. Had it lasted longer, she may have been tempted to rest her head, and her problems, on his strong shoulders.

Just once, to let herself lean on someone else.

"Come. Tell me about it." He seemed to read her mind as he nodded toward the porch swing. They climbed the steps and sat side by side.

"If my cousin wasn't already with our Chicago-based team, I'd try to snag her to come live in Refuge." But Mallory was engaged to a guy who wanted her in Chicago and uninvolved in Chloe's program.

Time to think of something more pleasant than how her cousin, her best friend, was about to ruin her life by marrying a man who'd make her forego her dreams. Projects and programs that Chloe and Mallory had planned since childhood.

Speaking of programs, Chloe studied Chance. Had he not been in the midst of difficulty, Chloe might've hit him up to be part of her southern Illinois team. Though he'd likely be willing, it would be too much to ask right now.

Then his plans to pursue youth pastoring passed through Chloe's mind again like a flesh-piercing arrow.

She scooted another inch away from him.

His long legs paused, the pressure pushing them in a relaxing back-and-forth swinging rhythm. He noticed.

She eyed her watch. "I should get to bed. I have back-to-back meetings tomorrow and a twelve-inch stack of papers to fill out for permissions and taxes, funding and zoning. Not to mention research on the citizens of Refuge to see if I can cull people to be on my team."

"I might be able to help with that if you tell me what you need."

Right now what she needed was for his cologne to stop overpowering her resistance to him.

She breathed deeply and wished breathing wasn't so necessary for survival. "I like what you wear."

He dipped his head to eye his T-shirt, emblazoned with a military emblem.

"I meant the woodsy cologne."

Her face heated about the time his shy grin appeared. "Thanks. You always smell good too." He bumped her shoulder with his, then left his arm resting against hers.

His nearness joined the cologne's assault on her senses. She could so easily fall for this man.

But falling in love right now was far too dangerous to her dreams. Chloe stood. "If you're serious about helping, come on inside."

She led him in and they sat around her lighted kitchen table. Chloe lost track of time, lost herself in him and in the number of cups of coffee and time they spent bent over her table going through the phone book and her required steps for the Refuge clinic. She chattered and Chance listened and occasionally offered suggestions. Good ones.

Had Chance not been beside her, calming and encouraging at the helm of every obstacle and challenge that surfaced in her search for solutions, she might have thrown up her hands. Her cell phone chimed. When she saw it was after eleven o'clock, alarm shot through her.

"Chloe, this is Fiona's mom. We're at the hospital."

"But the baby's not due for another five months!"

"She's in preterm labor. They've stopped it but said since the baby dropped, she'll be on bed rest for the duration of the pregnancy."

"Do you need me to come there? Can I do anything to help?"

"No, I think we have everything under control. Except that Fiona needs to rest, and she wouldn't until we called you. I know it's late, and I'm so sorry, but she wanted me to let you know she needs a medical leave of absence from the team."

Chloe's heart dipped, both from fear for her friend and her baby and because this would set Chloe back even more. If she had to keep putting out fires on her Chicago team, she couldn't focus on building Refuge's.

But truly, some things took precedence. People were more important than programs, period. Saving Fiona's baby's life was far more important. "Tell her not to worry at all. I'll take care of it and cover her duties. Tell her also that I'm praying."

"Thanks, Chloe. We knew you'd understand."

Chloe hung up and just sat there, staring. Then she pressed her fingertips to her pulsing temples and released them with an overdue sigh.

Chance sat beside her. "I take it something happened."

"Yeah. My best animal trainer on the Chicago rescue team is down for the count. Hospitalized with a problematic pregnancy. Please pray for the baby to go full-term?"

"Sure. Anything else?"

"Yes. Pray I can replace her quickly, and with someone very efficient. Otherwise, I will have to go back to Chicago."

A weaker woman would have given up and gone back to Chicago right then. But Chloe was no quitter.

Chance rested a hand on her back. His presence sustained her, especially when she realized he was praying right then and there.

After he finished, a sense of well-being catalyzed Chloe. Vigor renewed, she pulled out her planning board.

Chance handed her dry-erase markers as she plotted her plans and needs. Despite his upbeat attitude, the more she wrote the more she became overwhelmed. Discouragement took stabs at her. She girded her courage and pressed on.

Untold minutes ticked by. "I'm getting tired. Maybe I need a break." That whole quitting thing suddenly seemed appealing. But Chance's enthusiasm over her program catapulted her on. As Chloe researched, more urgent needs and time-consuming tasks emerged.

"My to-do list is about a mile long," Chloe groaned.

An owl hooted outside. Chance rose and stretched. Then he eyed his watch. "It's nearly midnight, and I've got an early class in the morning with new recruits. If I didn't have to get up before the birds, I'd stay longer. I need to chat with Brock a minute if he's still up and grab a few things from his place before I go." He offered her an apologetic glance, which is when she remembered she had his jacket still draped over her shoulders.

She went to remove it, but he shook his head. "I like the way it looks on you better."

She brushed fingers along the dark denim, enjoying the rugged-but-soft texture. "Are you saying I can keep it?"

He smiled a slightly sad grin as a flash of nostalgia

drifted like a sideways sunset across his handsome face.

"For a while, but not forever. It was the last gift Mom gave me before she died, or I'd let you have it."

Her hand fell to his arm. "I'm so sorry."

"Thanks. I know you've been there."

She nodded. Swallowed back lumps. How had she come to care for this man already? Frightening. Not having words for once in her life, she nodded and her bangs slipped from behind her ear.

His vision drifted there and for a moment he seemed mesmerized. His hand moved as though to brush them back off her forehead, but his fingers curled into his hand.

She couldn't deny the disappointment flooding her.

But it was for the best that they didn't act on this emotional attraction. If they did, it would be a detriment to her dreams. She moved so her chair sat safely between them, creating a physical barrier like the one she was trying to keep in place in her heart.

"I'll see you and Ivan tomorrow afternoon," she said in her best professional tone. It must have fallen short because he dipped his head and grinned. The way his dimples seemed to wink at her, maddening! Flustered with herself, Chloe grabbed her papers and went into an organizing frenzy.

His grin only widened as he knelt to pet Midnight, then ventured slowly toward her door. He paused halfway and peered back at her. His eyes said he didn't want to go. Her heart answered that cry with a squeeze and made her glad he took his time getting to the door. "See you tomorrow."

"Looking forward to it." Chance's stuttering had waned the more time he'd spent in her presence. "Let's do this again sometime. Often as we can."

His kindness gave her something to look forward to. "I'd like that." She reached to shake his hand. "As friends."

He ignored her hand and stared deeply into her eyes. "I like being with you, Chloe."

Don't say it back. Don't.

Hand snaking back to her side, she bit her lip against the sentiment trying to burst from her throat. If she admitted out loud that she liked being with him too, she might be tempted to let this fly like a fighter jet beyond the runway of friendship.

And she just couldn't. Not with her dreams just within reach.

She felt adrift when he turned away and walked into Brock's unit. The air around her grew empty and filled with loneliness.

She crossed her arms over herself and rested her hands along his jacket's sleeves. Then she tilted her head down and breathed in his manly scent evident in the traces of woodsy cologne. Powerful, like the draw that had pulled his eyes to hers while he took reluctant steps away. Though he couldn't possibly see in the window, she noticed that he cast glances over his shoulder, like he hadn't wanted to end their time together.

She could relate.

After one last, lingering glance her way, he closed Brock's door behind him.

Chloe remained on alert after Chance left, waiting to hear him emerge from Brock's unit. What seemed like hours later, footsteps sounded on the boardwalk. Was she imagining that they paused outside her door?

Chloe took a step, nearly stumbled over Midnight, sleeping in his bed beneath the window, and watched Chance walk to his car. He must still be in the process of moving. He had armfuls of clothes and teetering stacks of books. Titles she recognized as global best-sellers, as well as famous classics.

He was an avid reader? This big, bad Special Ops soldier? There were so many layers to this man. "*Special* is right." She sighed and closed her blinds so she didn't feel like a stalker spying on him as he loaded the Jeep.

Since Chance seemed to do a lot with Brock, that meant she'd no doubt see Chance more than antici-pated. She'd also see him while working with Ivan, but that was a professional environment. Here at Evie's B&B she could be more casual, friendlier.

Chance had said his dad wasn't typically this diffi-cult, but that using Midnight might not work. In such cases, Chloe didn't push the issue of animals in her therapy.

But Chloe felt in her gut that Midnight could help Ivan far faster and better than if she only used tradi-tional therapy.

Ivan was already in jeopardy of it being too late,

too long after the stroke to do much good as far as regaining dexterity and mobility.

Chloe yawned and rubbed her temples. It had been a long day, filled with a roller coaster of emotions. Chance's unexpected friendship and her attraction to him. Fiona's medical emergency. The complications with planning her program in Refuge. She headed toward her bedroom, knowing she needed to get some sleep so she could tackle whatever challenges the morning would bring.

The next evening, after a long grueling day of errands related to building her Refuge program, Chloe sat down with Ivan's chart. His therapy had brightened her day, even though Ivan had been a real pill through it and refused most of her new exercises.

Complicating matters, she'd been disappointed not to see Chance. Ivan said he'd taken a new recruit to lunch because the recruit had asked about Chance's church. That Chance had chosen to go to lunch rather than see her during Ivan's session needled her, even though she knew her reaction was ridiculous.

Her fax machine bleeped and she approached it. Good. Ivan's physician faxed her more of his history.

She kicked off her shoes, grabbed a pear and sat at the small kitchen table Evie had furnished.

Midnight lay down on top of her feet.

"Hmm. Ivan likes to work with clay. He has an Internet business and sells custom-made chess sets online. Let's check them out, Midnight. What do you think?" While Midnight chased a katydid across the floor, Chloe went online.

Images of beautifully handcrafted games appeared. Chloe set down her fruit. "Wow. He is really talented."

Empathy flooded her when a message appeared that said: "Due to family emergencies, we are unable to process orders at this time. We apologize for any inconvenience. Please check back next season."

"So sad." Chloe determined that minute to get Ivan to the point where he could work on his chess sets again.

More pictures scrolled across the screen. Chloe's heart melted at the images of family and friends that came in and out of focus with the slide show.

"That must be Ivan's late wife. Chance has his mom's smile." Speaking of Chance, image after image of him rolled across the screen. Some recent, some not.

"Wow. Ivan is really proud of his son." She wondered if Chance knew all these photos were on here.

She giggled at one of Chance holding a stringer of catfish. "He looks about ten years old here. And severely sunburned."

Another image scrolled. Chance in full dress blues. "Wow. Air Force guy. I must admit, he is so handsome he takes my breath away."

The next image caused her face to flush. Must be recent because it was Chance, looking similar to now, on a lake in a fishing boat with Brock.

She leaned in, very close. They were both shirtless and standing in camouflage shorts flexing ballooned biceps, washboard bellies and goofy grins.

She cleared her throat and grabbed papers off the table, then proceeded to fan herself furiously with them.

Thankfully, he was not shirtless in the next few photos. Those big, bulky guys must be part of his team. *PJs* or *Pararescue Jumpers,* Mandy had called them.

She'd look *pararescue* up after perusing Ivan's site and chart and formulating a written game plan. Images on the family-owned business site caused even more compassion to well up.

"Midnight, good buddy, we really have to work on Ivan. Okay? Starting tomorrow, let's do our best to help him get as much of his life back as possible."

The dog licked her hand, which she normally wouldn't allow. But she hadn't paid much attention to him today.

Giggling, Chloe got down on the living room floor and played until they were both worn out. Then she took him for his evening walk and readied for bed.

She wrestled with her pillow. Flopped, tossed, turned. The more she thought about Ivan and Chance and the family photos and all they'd lost when they lost Chance's mother and Ivan suffered his stroke, the more sleep eluded her. Turning her pillow to the cool side didn't help.

Ivan's Web site had given her intimate glimpses into their lives. And the Pararescue Jumpers site gave her a peek into the life of Chance, a true hero. The man who was becoming frighteningly intriguing to her and who felt far too familiar and fascinating for the little time they'd spent together.

And it seemed clear that the interest ran both ways.

Certainly the attraction did because she caught him checking her out every time she turned around, the same way she did him when he wasn't looking, which wasn't often.

This man was a rare breed. One who was, as their pararescue creed stated, willing to risk his life for others. The creed scrolled through her mind and left her more unsettled.

It is my duty as a pararescueman to save life and aid the injured. I will be prepared at all times to perform my assigned duties quickly and efficiently, placing these duties before personal desires and comforts. These things I do, "That Others May Live."

That creed also meant he'd never give up his duty for any woman. Not even his wife. Just like her dad, his career would always come first.

Nevertheless, her determination to be involved in this family was about Ivan, not about Chance and not about her. She must really be tired. Otherwise her brain wouldn't have brought the ridiculous and very premature concept of marriage into the mix.

If Ivan didn't start rehabbing soon, he'd never regain use of his hand, which meant he'd never build his beloved chess sets again.

This case was time sensitive, and she owed Mandy a major favor. More than that, she'd come to care for Ivan.

Ivan had been worse than ever in his resistance this week. But that only fed her dogged determination. Even though time with Chance's father cut severely into her planning and research time, plus the other work she needed to do to launch the animal-assisted therapy program proposal.

Chloe shook her head and punched her fist into her pillow, trying to get comfortable. No matter what opposition bounded in her path, she was determined not to let anything prevent her from going back. Slowly, she closed her eyes, plans marching across her vision as she drifted off to sleep.

Chapter Five

She was back.

With dogzilla.

And an armful of flowers so large they camouflaged her lovely face.

Chance was floored to find his dad's neck craning to see the bouquet ambling up the drive. He had expected to meet his dad's fury. Instead, he wore a slight, lopsided grin. "She came back again? Gutsy, that girl."

Chance smiled as he reached to get the door for the lovely person God had sent to answer his most desperate prayer: that Ivan would snap out of his grief-driven depression enough to try to physically rehabilitate.

He knew Dad well enough to know that when he snapped back from the crushing blow of losing his soul mate, he'd regret not working harder to regain use of his limbs.

Chance swung the door open to see her vivacious

grin, an expression that made his heart feel as if it hit a trip wire.

"Hey, soul-ja boy. Take this." She plopped a large paper bag in his arms, not pausing to see if he'd protest.

Soul-ja? Maybe he wouldn't tell her just yet that technically he was an Airman and not a Soldier. He rather liked the way the title rolled off her tongue.

Pleasant smells wafted from the bag, warm against his skin. He peeked. "You bought dinner?" Surprise streaked through him. His mouth moistened and his tummy rumbled.

"Nope. I *made* dinner. I *bought* the foam since you two bachelors seem hesitant to part with it."

Surprisingly, the "bachelor" statement didn't seem to upset his dad. Only because the smell of delicious barbecue had no doubt reached Ivan's eager nose.

"Hello again," she said to Ivan and set her medical bag on the folding chair near the door. Chance really needed to get the rest of Ivan's furniture in here.

She placed the vibrant flowers on the coffee table in a vase she tugged from her bottomless bag.

Just how much sunshine could one girl bring?

Chloe approached Ivan and chattered like they were old friends, even though Ivan had vowed to banish her after their last session, when she'd apparently pushed Ivan to bump up his strength training.

Chance's gaze veered to Midnight, who had accompanied her in and who now watched Chance carefully, soulfully. Vying for trust and affection. Chance's gaze snagged on something, echoes of fear embedded deep in the dog's dark, cavernous eyes.

Then the mutt's mouth relaxed into a friendly pant that made him look like he was laughing. His eyes livened as they sought Chloe. The dog obviously loved and trusted her with his whole being.

Ivan might not have a soft spot for animals, but Chance sure did. He had the sudden urge to pet Midnight, but didn't suppose he should with the dog being on duty.

Dog on duty. In his dad's house. His dad, the antidog person. Chance wanted to laugh at the absurd twist of fate. Chloe seemed to have Ivan wrapped around her slender fingers, despite Ivan's steely resistance. No wonder Mandy hadn't elaborated on what she meant about Chloe being unconventional.

Chloe cast a glance over her shoulder, proving her eyes were truly as green-yet-golden and her hair as glistening as his dreams convinced him of last night. "Can you take care of drinks? Otherwise dinner might get cold."

"I'll pour us water." Then he'd brew after-dinner tea.

After they'd eaten the delicious lunch of Chloe's barbecued spare ribs, Chance stepped from the room to give her a chance to rebuild critical rapport with his dad without feeling like Chance stood over her shoulder.

Three minutes.

That's all it had taken her to gain Chance's full trust. For that's all the time it took her to get Ivan to run through the neurological and strength checks that the hospital rehab team couldn't coax out of him in three weeks.

Chance stood in the kitchen of the tiny house that he'd rented for his dad and himself and slowly moved them into over the past weekends, much to Ivan's protest. But his doctors had said he could no longer live alone, and Chance couldn't bear sending him to a nursing home.

Chance reached for the teakettle, then froze when memories poured into his head. Steeped in sentiment, he studied the kettle and smiled as memory after happy memory slid through his mind. The forgotten images of his mom were an unexpected gift from God in the midst of grief that would have ground him into dust if the strong sense of God's presence and mercy hadn't accompanied them.

The kettle had been Mom's for years. She had it as far back as he could remember. The dings, dents and faded design evidenced how old it was. How she'd loved it. Used it.

Wow. He missed her.

What I wouldn't give for another day.

His throat knotted and his fingers quivered slightly as he grasped the handle that her hands had so often held when serving tea for the never-ending stream of guests in their home. His mom had a gift of hospitality. People warmed easily to her. She had a welcoming way about her. Most importantly, she could talk Ivan into anything.

Chloe reminded Chance of her in that way.

Feeling suddenly steeped too long in loss, he shoved the memories asunder, tucked them away for later, and put water on to boil.

The last thing he wanted was to waver on a crumbling ledge of emotion. Nausea accosted him.

Combat nature rising up to take a militant stand, Chance mouthed a sustaining scripture, clenched his fist and turned his attention away from stark sadness and toward the kettle. Focusing on others fought self-pity.

The combined antidotes of faith and fortitude worked.

What would Chloe want? What would Mom choose for her? Chance looked around the cupboards. There. Decided. He opened the package of blooming tea and put the lump near the glass pitcher. Maybe the bloom would impress Chloe.

Alone in the kitchen, Chance smiled.

Mandy had informed him when she'd arrived to sit with Ivan yesterday that Chloe was a tea and flower fanatic.

Why he wanted to impress her was beyond him, but he did. Tea on task, he stepped toward the doorway to watch them unobserved. Mandy and his other teammates' wives had dropped by Evie's to welcome Chloe to Refuge. And they had evidently filled Chloe in on tidbits of Chance's life. Had Chloe asked for the information? Or had his teammates' good-hearted, meddling, matchmaking wives offered the info unsolicited?

Chance studied Chloe and wished he knew.

The teakettle whistled. He set it aside and shut off the burner before returning to the doorway leading from the kitchen to the living room.

A familiar smell caught him off guard. Chloe pulled a glass pan from her bag that smelled suspiciously like the banana-split cake his mother always used to make for Ivan because it was his favorite dessert. And Chance's.

Without thinking, he drifted toward the smell.

Giggling took his attention from the cake she set on the coffee table. Chloe. Her laugh was like emotional tech support. He dialed in.

Ivan gave a *harrumph* and leaned on his four-pronged cane. "I don't eat any woman's dessert except for my wife's." But Ivan licked his lips as he eyed the cake.

Chloe giggled again, then feigned offense by plopping balled fists on her hips. "Why not? Most people who eat my food live to tell about it."

Ivan looked like he wanted to laugh at that but pressed his lips together. "Furthermore, I never heard tell of any kinda legit therapist using animals."

Chloe grinned then mimicked his dad's scowl.

"I sure wouldn't want that thing running around shedding all over everything," his dad continued.

"I'll make sure my *assistant* doesn't shed in your home." Now Chloe looked close to laughing.

Ivan looked like a bullfrog puffing to the point of *poof.* "This ain't my home!"

"Is that right?" she said a smidgen too pleasantly, as though spurring his father on in his rant. Was she trying to get him riled enough to come out of the chair and kick her and Cujo out? Or was this one of the unconventional therapist's stealthy maneuvers Mandy had raved about?

Either she was a complete ditz or a compelling genius.

Which one? He observed Chloe carefully.

She pulled an RC Cola out of her bag, then quickly popped the tab and set it near Ivan's strong arm. He picked the can up. Chloe set her bag on his table, covering it so nothing could be placed there, and extended a piece of cake.

Chance smiled.

Without thinking, Ivan reached with his affected arm for the piece of cake she extended, and Chance realized she was tricking him into using his weaker muscles.

"Yes. That's right," Ivan ranted, still not realizing he held the cake in his weak hand. It was the first time since the stroke he'd gripped something for that long a period.

A huge wave of relief rushed over Chance when he realized what was going on. No ditz here.

Chloe was not only a genius but a stealthy one.

Just how did she know his dad loved RC Cola and banana-split cake? He'd find out her sources and thank them. How he'd missed that sweet dessert, but more so the woman who loved to make it, then watch her "boys" eat it. *Mom.*

Chance's eyes and throat burned.

If she were here, she could get Dad to do his exercises. But the fact that she was gone was the reason Ivan wouldn't. Dad didn't want to go on without her. But Chance was determined to make him, because one day life without her would hold hope again.

Chloe coming back today was the first spark of it that he'd seen in Ivan's eyes since the funeral, proving he'd also secretly feared Chloe wouldn't return.

Her face lit with humor as his father jabbed a crooked finger toward Chance as he now stepped into view. "He moved me out against my will and stuck me here in this dumb little over-carpeted domino box."

Ivan gestured toward Midnight and slanted his eyebrows toward the tip of his nose. "And that's no assistant. That's nothing but a goofy-looking, web-footed bird hound." He bent his head toward the dog's paws. "Why, look. He ain't even growed into his feet yet."

Ivan eyed Chloe and cocked his head to the side which, because of the nerve damage caused by the stroke, could have been menacing or comical depending on which side of Dad's face one stood on.

"What's he doing here anyway? Besides getting zillions of pokey hairs all over the ugly floor?" Ivan asked.

In truth, Chance agreed with that.

What kind of therapist used pets in their work? His bushy tail, wagging a hundred times a second, was weapon enough to sweep knickknacks off shelves should the dog decide to take an uninvited stroll through the place.

Chloe knelt and scrubbed Midnight beneath the chin. The warm, loving look she issued the dog made him envy the mutt for the affection. "Time to show off what you've got."

Midnight stepped toward Ivan, rested his chin on Ivan's knee and sighed like they were the best of friends.

Ivan stilled. Seconds ticked by, and then Ivan's face lit. "Say, he reminds me of a dog I had when I was just a pup." Ivan got a sweet, reminiscent look in his eyes.

Suddenly, Chance saw. Clearly. There was way more therapy going on here than met the eye.

He looked at the therapist in a new light. All of a sudden, so did his father as he caught Chance observing Chloe. Was the room's recessed lighting playing tricks on him, or did a flash of momentary amusement just enter Dad's new lopsided expression?

Midnight inched closer to Ivan, who returned his attention to the dog. "Mangy mutt. That's what you are." But less bite resided in Ivan's bark this time.

Midnight was far from mangy. His glistening coat and eyes and muscular build spoke of spectacular care and healthy helpings of food and exercise. Chance knew a thriving animal when he saw one. Midnight didn't have a dirty hair on his slick, black body.

After polishing off the cake and RC, Ivan shifted in his recliner. The pencil Chance had earlier placed on his chair-side table rolled onto the floor.

Chloe whispered a command. Midnight picked up the pencil and placed it back on the table. Ivan's eyes lit and he started to grin, until he noticed Chance and Chloe watching. He reverted to scowling again. If his arm would work right, Chance was sure he would cross them staunchly over his barrel chest.

"Hmph. Happenstance." Ivan leaned over and bumped the table with his quad cane until the pencil rolled off again.

With merely a nod from Chloe, Midnight picked up the pencil and placed it farther back on the table.

"S-smart dog," Chance said, hating the stutter that came back when he least expected it.

If Chloe noticed, she didn't show it.

"Sure is. Aren't ya, buddy?" The pretty, warm smile she doled out to the dog ramped Chance's pulse. Suddenly, that was reason enough to want her gone. Or to be gone himself.

"I'll check on the tea." Chance started to step from the room, but Chloe's gaze raised swiftly and sharply. The intent, imploring look she sent Chance arrested his stride. She rose and placed in Ivan's strong hand the leash attached to Midnight's chest harness.

Ivan grunted his protest, but Chloe kept her confident stride and left Ivan's side.

What did she think she was doing, leaving her dog near a disabled, disgruntled man who so apparently wanted nothing to do with it? Chance wondered.

As if reading his question, Chloe mouthed out of Ivan's eyeshot, "Trust me."

Ivan's mouth, or the one unaffected side of it, gaped as she stepped toward Chance, now feet away from escaping via the kitchen.

"Say! Come back here. What am I supposed to do with this?" Ivan protested.

Midnight let out a soft *woof!*

"I'm letting you mind him for me while I talk to Chance about the treatment plan."

Was she talking to his dad or the dog? Chance couldn't be sure. Both looked equally concerned about her departure. Midnight moved into a protective stance near Ivan, as though guarding him from harm. He also eyed the pencil, ready to retrieve it should it fall again on his watch.

At the door, Chloe smiled at Ivan. "I'll just be a moment with your son. If you need something, ding the bell on Midnight's collar and he'll come get me."

Because Chance had been a late-in-life baby, most people mistook his parents to be his grandparents. It was something that always irritated Ivan. Chance warmed another degree toward Chloe because she hadn't slipped and said *grandson*.

"Wait. What bell?" Ivan looked worried about being left alone, a common fear since the stroke, especially since the doctor told him if he wasn't compliant with treatment and therapy, he could have another one.

Chloe must have sensed the fear. Face softening, she returned to Ivan's side immediately. "It's right under here." She pointed to the bell beneath Midnight's chin, which is when Chance noticed the scars.

Scars that looked like tears or gashes.

What on earth? Had Midnight been attacked by another animal? Sure looked like it. What had that poor dog endured with those injuries? But Midnight seemed well cared for and healthy now, physically and emotionally.

Chloe patted the dog, then faced her palm to his nose. "Stay."

Midnight looked for a split second like he wanted to tackle her and lick her half to death, but instead he pulled his panting tongue in and stiffened obediently, like a dutiful soldier during roll call.

Wow. Impressive. She had excellent dog-handling skills. "Good dog," Chance said.

Midnight's gaze veered to him and for a second he looked like he wanted to rush Chance and finagle a few pats and clandestine nuzzles. But he only moved a fraction before his gaze snapped back to Chloe. Then he swung his massive head around to keep careful watch on Ivan and the persnickety pencil.

Midnight only removed his gaze long enough to watch Chloe intently as she met Chance near the kitchen door. "Keep an eye on him while we talk in here a moment."

Again, Chance wasn't sure whether she was talking to the dog or Dad, but when she looped her arm through his elbow and tugged him into the kitchen as if she'd known him for ages, he felt momentarily stripped of speech. If he said anything right now, he'd undoubtedly stutter.

They parted and Chloe squealed. He whirled, wondering if she'd seen the little mouse who hadn't wanted to move out when Chance and his dad moved in.

But she was staring at the stove. "Is that blooming tea? For *me?*" Her voice reminded him of a little kid excited over the biggest present under the tree.

He grinned and poured the hot water in a glass pitcher then dropped the bulb into it. Chloe moved close enough that her elbow brushed his, courtesy of the small counter space, as they watched the flowering tea bulb bloom.

Might be his imagination, but as the tea flower slowly opened, it seemed something bloomed further between him and Chloe too. As if thinking the same, she turned to study him. "I've never met a guy who knew what blooming tea was. You're something else, Chance Garrison. You know that?"

He shrugged. "The tea was Mom's. So I h-hope it's not stale. She always entert-tained her Vault ladies with it."

"Vault ladies?" Chloe tilted her face. He enjoyed the shape of her profile at that angle, or any angle really.

"Yeah, sh-she used to host a women's p-prayer group in her home. The ladies named it the Vault b-because th-they knew when they told Mom something, she'd keep it locked in confidence forever."

"So is your whole family Christian?"

Chance nodded. "Yeah, my p-parents have been but I only recently committed. I haven't been able to get Dad to go to church since Mom died though."

"He'll come around."

"I hope so." Chance eyed her, noticing she didn't elaborate on her own faith, or lack thereof. Interesting.

He headed to the table to pull out a chair for her, but she tiptoed back to the door. Putting a silencing finger to her mouth, she inched near the crack and motioned him close.

Chance complied. At six feet tall, he stood about six inches above her head. Sweet strawberry scents wafted toward him and he had to consciously keep himself from breathing deeper since his nose was close to her silky hair.

He never liked strawberries more than in this moment.

"Look," she whispered, awestruck.

Chance trailed her gaze to find Dad still grumbling, yet reaching with his affected arm to begrudgingly pet the dog, who continually nudged his hand with gentle affection-seeking motions.

Overwhelmed with what he was seeing and realizing what she'd accomplished, Chance pulled her around by the shoulders and looked at her with what he knew was the same expression those he rescued from harm always wore.

"Amazing. You just tricked him into doing his hand exercises, didn't you?"

"Amazing," she echoed teasingly. "You *are* as smart as the cupid posse says."

"Huh?"

She grinned. "Celia, Amber and Mandy talk nonstop about you."

"W-wh—"

"You catch on quick," she whispered and winked. Not only that, she patted a gentle hand along his cheek and turned back to watching Ivan through the crack.

He'd figure out the meaning of her words later. Right now, he focused on the lovely shape of the mouth that spoke them. The warmth of her smile and the feel of her hand on his face. The smell of strawberry-scented hair inches away. It all reminded him of just how long it had been since he'd had the pleasure of holding a beautiful woman in his arms.

Chance had put aside any thoughts of romance or relationships since his mom died and his dad became ill. He was dedicated to helping his dad rehabilitate, and he knew he had some of his own emotional healing to do. Those things—and his duties as a PJ— were his priorities for now. Because the last thing Chance wanted was to lose the parent he had left.

Therefore, the last thing Chance needed was to be interested in a lady.

So he should forget how mesmerizing the unique gold spackles dotted through the deep green in her eyes were.

Instead, he found himself trying to memorize them.

Chapter Six

"I can't believe myself." Chloe shoved Midnight's pillow toward the center of her Suburban's passenger seat. "I've never acted so unprofessionally on the job."

Her attraction toward Chance that had flared without permission or warning traipsed through Chloe's mind like an insolent, taunting child.

"What bothers me most is my undoubtedly perceptible reaction to it and that, for the third time in my life, I was rendered speechless—a rare feat in itself."

Three out of three times that she could recall being speechless in her twenty-five years, and they all involved Chance. His nearness had jumbled her thoughts to the point she'd lost her train of speech.

She clicked her tongue in self-disgust and yanked the strap of the doggy seat belt across Midnight who, as usual, listened to her incessant banter with undying loyalty and a rapt expression.

She could probably say, "You're an oversize drool-ball with lanky legs," and as long as she smiled while she said it, he'd pant in perpetual contentment. But his even temperament was exactly what made him the perfect canine candidate for her animal-assisted therapy program.

Now, if she could only convince the good people of Refuge that such a program would be worthwhile here.

After securing Midnight, she climbed into the driver's seat and adjusted her visor. "Whew! Southern Illinois summers are way warmer than Chicago, boy. It's going to take some getting used to, huh?"

Feeling eyes on her besides Midnight's dark and devoted ones, she peered back toward the house.

Chance, looking lethally cute with feet squared and thumbs hooked through pockets of camouflage fatigues, stood on the porch watching her go. A flush crept from her neck to her cheeks and back. She waved bye.

A slow, shy smile carved an irresistible dimple into the edge of his generous mouth as his sturdy hand raised to bid her a chivalrous goodbye, as he stared at her appreciatively.

An automatic answering grin tried to wrestle its way to her traitorous mouth.

Fighting it with all the facial strength she could muster, Chloe nodded politely and responded with a stiff, professional nod even though her cheeks were about to explode from holding the erupting smile in.

Deep down, something in her had longed all of her adult life to have a man like that look at her that way.

Hands planted primly on the wheel, she pulled away from the curb and her urge to gawk at the beautiful man.

"Shew-wee, but he's cute!" She scrubbed Midnight behind the ears and eyed her phone. Two messages. One from Mallory, one from Mom. Chloe pulled over in a park and called her mom back since they were set to meet for dinner.

She sounded winded when she answered. "Hi, Chloe. I'll be running late. I'm still at work."

"Rough day?" Chloe rolled her window down and appreciated the fresh floral air and greenery of the park. Mom would melt over these vivid flowers. All in full bloom too. Hopefully, Mary would get her flower garden greenhouse up and running soon.

Even though Mandy would lose a good worker, they knew how much Mary missed growing bright plants to sell from her home-based florist business. Refuge-area nursing home patrons would benefit from the fresh flowers Mary was bound to take there on visits with Chloe and Midnight.

So much left to do before they could launch all of that.

In the meantime, her mom occupied herself and kept the bills paid by doing medical transcription.

"Two back-to-back emergency pediatric surgeries put us behind on paperwork. So I'm hanging around to help Dr. Manchester-Briggs out."

"Does Mandy know I met with the client she referred me to again today?"

"Yeah, she asked how it went. I'll let you talk to her." Her mother recited directions to the restaurant before passing the phone off to Mandy.

"Hey, Chloe. Did you meet Chance and his dad again?"

Why so much emphasis on Chance? Phooey. Probably her imagination. "Yes, and I brought Midnight again."

"How'd that go?"

"They didn't toss us out." Chloe laughed. "Although if Chance's dad was capable, he might have."

"Chance is a strong person. But I think losing another parent soon would just about do him in. He so badly wants his dad to get better. At the same time, he feels like the weak link of his team. He's having trouble eating and sleeping. The guys all understand."

"Sounds like he's pretty hard on himself." Why was Mandy discussing Chance rather than Ivan? Cupid posse on the loose, just like when Chloe had talked to Celia and Amber about bringing Midnight to visit their special-needs students. All they had done is gush about Chance.

"Yeah, he claims he can't keep everything together emotionally. But his drive to help his dad and be the best PJ he can is paramount and his faith steadfast."

Steadfast. Great attribute. Fitting for Chance.

"If there's one word to describe what I know of him so far and what I've learned about him from you and the cupi—er, his friends, steadfast is it."

"We all see it. I wish he did. How's Ivan?"

"Chance will work with him on exercises while I'm gone. Ivan agreed to comply as long as I keep bringing home-cooked meals."

"Awww! How sweet." Mandy giggled.

"I don't have anybody to cook for, so I don't mind. I like it."

"Maybe you'll help Chance get his appetite back."

For whatever reason, Chloe blushed. It had thrilled her when Chance had complimented her in his slow drawl. "He said he looks forward to sharing more of my food and my time after I return from Chicago. I have to go back to replace Fiona, my right hand in the program there. She is on bed rest in a high-risk pregnancy."

"I'm sorry to hear that, but how exciting that Chance likes to spend time with you."

"He could have been being polite."

"Or he could have been hinting at a date."

The thought thrust her brain into a tailspin and made her feel too warm and fuzzy for comfort. "Anyway, tell Mom I'll meet her at the restaurant. Feel free to join us."

"Thanks, maybe another time. I have a hot date with my hubby this evening. Joel, their team leader, encourages the married guys to have date nights with their spouses."

"That's smart, I suppose."

"Chance is one of the two single guys, by the way. Brock is the other one."

The neck flush returned to Chloe. Why would Mandy feel the need to point that out?

Chloe had no intention whatsoever of letting any ministry-minded man, no matter how enticing, push her dreams to the back burner, or worse, snuff them altogether.

Yep, best to forget the strapping PJ's piercing green eyes. Unlike her green with gold streaks, his were gold with green flecks. And she ought to be ashamed of herself for noticing that sort of thing while on the job.

Nope. She had no intention of following in her mother's footsteps and falling for a man consumed by his work, his faith or both.

One week later, footsteps pounded the boardwalk outside the B&B Friday evening as Chance waited for Brock to get out of the shower. He peered out the window to see a black flurry rushing past, dragging something that stumbled to keep up.

He opened the door. "Chloe?"

She tripped over bright skirts and hit the deck, legs and arms sprawled every which way. He rushed to her side.

She rolled over, moaned, then started laughing.

Midnight chased a cardinal off the white wrap-around porch rail. Chance offered Chloe a hand up and held her gaze with his. "Welcome back!" He nodded toward Midnight. "You know, he is a bird dog after all."

Chloe shook her head. "Thanks. And there are countless birds here. Unlike Chicago. He's not supposed to chase things, being a therapy dog, but he's still learning. Speaking of, I know better than to wrap his leash around my wrist. Ow!" She rubbed it.

The paramedic in him kicking in, Chance reached for her hand and turned it over to assess the angry red line the leash had burned into her delicate skin. He felt a spark run through him as he held her hand, but he tried to focus on her injury. "He's a strong dog. This is just a surface wound though. You'll be okay."

Because she seemed acutely uncomfortable with his touch, he released her wrist. "Try icing it."

She groaned at Midnight, now after a robin. "I'll never catch him at this rate."

She brushed a smoothing hand along the sundress that barely skimmed her knees. "Do you jog often?" Chance asked.

She turned from watching Midnight frolic in the yard and glanced quizzically at him. "Huh?"

"You have a runner's physique."

"Thanks, I think. But no. I exercise as little as humanly possible. The only running I do is after that hairy hooligan when he gets a notion to go after something feathered or furry."

Midnight must run off frequently then, because she had very shapely legs. He forced his eyes to retrain on her face. "How'd the trip go?"

Frustration fluttered across Chloe's face. "Not as well as I'd hoped. Fiona is doing okay, but she will remain on bed rest, and I only found a temporary replacement for her. Which reminds me, I have work to do. I'd better get going." She corralled Midnight with Chance's help and stepped into her unit.

Brock's door opened, and he poked his head out. Water droplets clung to his red hair. "What's the racket? Sounded like we were back dodging bombs in Baghdad."

Chance grinned. "Need you ask?"

"Chloe's back, and Midnight is after another squirrel?"

"Yep, she's back. And no squirrels. Birds this time." Chance followed Brock inside so he could finish getting ready. "Yo, you primp like a girl."

"That's because I'd like to get a girl."

"Well, don't get one with asthma unless you're packin' an arsenal of EpiPens, because all that cologne you've slathered on will send her into a deadly attack."

Laughing, Brock stepped in front of the hall mirror and slapped gel on his buzz so he could spike it. Chance grabbed a swig of high-pulp orange juice he'd left in the fridge while Brock searched in his closet, presumably for shoes.

Once outdoors, Chance eyed Chloe's door as they passed it to get to the steps. "Maybe we should invite her along."

Brock paused on the boardwalk. "Go for it. No one needs to sit home alone on a Friday night."

"She said she had work to do."

"So tell her she can do it later. We're going to the first show, then we'll grab a bite to eat. We can always bring her back early if she doesn't want to eat with us."

Hoping like crazy she would want to go, Chance rapped knuckles on Chloe's door.

It opened quickly. Her eyes and smile widened in pleasant surprise when she saw them. "Hey, guys." She peered around Brock at Chance. "What's going on?"

Chance clammed up.

Brock jabbed his ribs from the back.

"Uh, we w-were headed to the m-movies. Wanna c-come?"

She'd turn him down. He knew she would.

She turned to eye the papers on her table while nibbling her lip. "I suppose I could work on my stuff tomorrow morning." She refocused on Chance. "Sure. I'd love to." She grabbed her purse off the table, then stopped. "Oh, wait. I need to freshen up. Are we in a hurry?"

Chance laughed. "Unless you take as much time as Brock getting ready, we should be fine."

Giggling, she stepped back. "Come on in. I'll just be a minute."

Fifteen minutes later she emerged from putting on makeup and stood in front of the hallway mirror, fixing her hair. Chance lifted Midnight's leash from the coat tree. "I'll take him outside before we go."

Chloe snickered on her way to the bathroom. Chance wasn't sure why.

Brock walked with Chance around the yard while Midnight did his business. Every time he tried to chase whatever rustled in the bushes edging the woods, Chance pulled up on his leash and issued a firm "No."

Moments later Chloe came outside. Wow, her efforts to spruce herself up were certainly worth it. Chance realized he was gawking again when Brock wrestled the leash from his hands so a bright-eyed Chloe could put the dog inside. Both with her vividly hued makeup and without, she was breathtakingly beautiful.

"He didn't try to run off?" She looked at Chance.

"He tried." Chance studied her in return.

"He didn't get loose?" Arched eyebrows drew inward.

"Nope."

"Wow. He listens to you better than me."

So that's why she'd snickered earlier. She'd expected Midnight to drag him through the woods. Chance grinned and felt a touch of pride, especially when respect escalated in her eyes.

Small victory.

She tucked a purse under her arm. "Ready?"

During the evening, Brock left an open place beside Chloe so Chance could sit next to her. Chance owed his buddy, big-time.

They opted to watch a comedy rather than an action flick since Chloe said she loved to laugh, which suited Chance because he loved to hear her.

He enjoyed watching her more than the movie. She even let him buy popcorn and soda for her. Of course, he paid for Brock's too, since he guilted Chance into it. That made Chloe laugh again, which definitely made the twenty bucks for refreshments worth it. Afterward, the three went to enjoy a hearty dinner at the authentic Mexican restaurant near Manny's.

The owner's children entered with their mother just after Chance, Chloe and Brock sat down. "She had them later in life, like Mom had me," Chance said as the woman shuffled in and sighed.

"She looks pretty winded," Brock noted as the kids took off and their mom tried unsuccessfully to catch them before they dashed into the kitchen.

The owner carried the children out and sat with his wife.

"They both look haggard, like it's too much for them to keep up with their youngsters' energetic demands." Compassion for the family filled Chance. "Exactly why I want kids while I'm young."

He didn't miss the way Chloe's face pinched. "There are also drawbacks to having kids while you're young, you know."

Chance nodded. "I guess it's all a matter of preference."

"I'm definitely not having kids when I'm young." She dabbed her mouth with a napkin and watched the children who tried to drag their parents up from sitting. The parents looked extremely exhausted, like they needed a two-day nap.

Memories resurfaced of his own parents' inability to play sports or games or anything that required much physical activity. Chance clenched his jaw.

He wanted a family while he was young. And he would not relent on that. He wanted to be the best dad possible to his children, and he wanted his wife to be healthy and energetic.

Everyone on his team knew he was on the hunt for a wife, but he wasn't in a hurry to get the wrong one.

Chance's vision slipped from the family to Chloe

who smiled kindly at the fatigued parents and waved playfully at the children.

While he was attracted to her and even saw her as someone he could possibly fall in love with and marry, he knew there were obstacles. She was ambitious, and she'd just made it very clear where she stood on having children while she was young. Still, he wondered how adamant she was about that.

"Mmm. So good." Chloe licked enchilada sauce off her fingers. Chance paused midbite. His throat dried and his pulse ramped up a notch. Wanting his mind to honor God rather than linger on her lips, he diverted his attention to his plate.

And surprisingly found it empty.

He couldn't recall another time in the last six months when he'd polished off an entire meal. But he had eaten every bite of this one during the course of being immersed in conversation with Chloe.

Brock noticed because he eyed Chance's plate, then Chloe, and grinned. Slowly and smugly. Yet gratefully. Chance recognized the appreciation in Brock's brown, introspective eyes. Same way Chance felt.

His team loved and lived like brothers. When one suffered, they all did and rallied in undying support. When one celebrated, the entire team went all out to share it.

Yeah, way more therapy going on than he'd planned for. Chloe was like Midas to gold. She brightened everyone she touched.

Which meant trouble, real trouble to his heart if it ever went into a free fall and hers stayed grounded.

Chapter Seven

She was in real trouble. She'd had a great time last night with Chance. Well, Brock too. But it was obvious by his attention that Chance was the one interested in her.

And as much as she didn't want to be, she was interested right back. More than once she'd found herself wishing Chance would try to hold her hand during the movie or steal a kiss at the end of the evening. If Brock hadn't been there, would he have?

It didn't help that the movie had been a romantic comedy. Her phone trilled, jolting her from her reverie. Mallory's number appeared on the caller ID.

"So…who were you at dinner with when I called last night?" was the first question out of her cousin's mouth.

Chloe laughed. "I knew you'd be asking if you heard their voices in the background."

"Their? More than one?"

"Yeah, it was a friendship outing."

"Why?"

Chloe laughed. "Because I need friends and I think they picked up on that."

"Too bad. You need a boyfriend more. So who was the one with the rocker dude, deep DJ voice?"

"That was Brock."

"Sounds cute."

Wow. It had been a long time since Mallory had mentioned a guy other than her fiancé in a positive light. Could something be going on in Mal's relationship?

"He is very cute." *Cuter than your fiancé. Nicer too.* "But the other one's cuter." Though Mal would probably disagree since they had very different taste in men. "He's more the quiet observer, so you probably didn't hear him. He's adorably shy."

"Hmm. Does shy guy have a name?"

"Chance Garrison."

"Garrison. Related to Ivan, your one and only human patient at present?"

"Yep. His son. The other guy was his friend, and he's very single and avidly looking."

A pause. "I'm taken."

"I know." Chloe also knew hesitation when she heard it. And it definitely preceded Mal's declaration.

"I want to hear more about this shy guy. Did he buy?"

"Yes. Dinner, a big tub of popcorn, soda and a movie."

"So he seems interested?"

"I think so."

A high-pitched squeal came through the phone that Chloe knew was Mal but sounded like her pot-bellied pig, Penelope. "Go for it!"

"Are you crazy? Romance is the last thing I need right now."

"You big chicken."

"Cluck-cluck."

That evoked images of Mallory's dream wedding since she wanted her rescue animals to be a part of it.

They'd agreed to be each other's maids of honor since childhood. But enough talk about marriage. Talking made her think about it for herself, and that day was far, far away.

"You still dreaming of an animal-themed wedding?"

Mallory sighed. "Yeah. Haven't managed to talk Bert into it yet."

"I hate to break it to you, but I doubt you ever will." Or that Bert would actually go through with walking down the aisle at all. That could be a blessing for Mal, who'd hopefully see his true colors before the vows.

"So why aren't you interested in this Garrison guy?" Mallory asked.

"Because, like my dad, he's married to his job. It would be the mistress of our lives."

"You're so dramatic."

"It's true. He has a very important career and not one that could be worked around my schedule. So he's out as far as potentials. Although I'm flabbergasted and flattered he's attracted to normal old me. He's quite the hero." Chloe sighed.

"You, fan of neon-green everything, eighties earrings and flamboyant hippie-style geometric dresses? You're nowhere near normal, Chloe." Mallory giggled.

"Ha-ha. He doesn't seem to mind my eccentricity."

"Then you should reconsider. The suits you date always try to put you back in the box, and that's not where you belong. If shy guy likes you the way you are, you should give him a shot."

"Tell you what, you heed my advice on men and I'll heed yours."

"Ha." Mal snapped her gum. "On that note, I'll let you go. Don't forget, conference call Tuesday with the team."

"I won't. Speaking of, how's Fiona's replacement working out?"

Another pause. "I'm covering for Mindy quite a bit because she's in school. Bert's not thrilled about it."

"I'm sorry, Mal. I don't want the program to put tension in your relationship." Much as Chloe didn't care for Bert, she did care for Mal. "Do I need to return to Chicago?" The thought of not seeing Chance sent a wave of disappointment through her. Dread over what would become of Ivan crashed behind it.

"Not right now. I'll manage."

"You sure?" Mal didn't sound convincing.

Chloe felt equally torn between Chicago and Refuge.

"Yeah, for now. Let's hope Mindy can stay longer."

"Okay. Bye, Mal." Chloe hung up, glad for the reminder to get her notes together for the call. Everyone attending had questions she'd need to answer, and rather than complete their questionnaires she'd gone to town with Chance and Brock, although that had been way more fun.

She pulled out the paperwork and went down the list of people on her Chicago team. She'd need to construct an identical second team of people either from Refuge or willing to relocate to the area. But she wanted to give the people of Refuge first shot at the positions.

So far, she had twelve openings to fill. She couldn't do that until the city council gave her clearance.

Two hours later, Chloe's head pounded from the stress of all she had to do in so little time, plus all that would have to be accomplished, all the people and things that would have to line up and fall into place for this program to get off the ground and succeed long-term.

Her first hurdle was talking the small, old-fashioned town leaders into trying something so progressive.

The tune to the television show featuring Andy Griffith and Mayberry went through her mind, and she chuckled, remembering the small town featured in the old black-and-white series. Nevertheless, she loved it here and appreciated the ability to look out her window and see soybean fields and corn blowing in the breeze while animals frolicked in the outlying woods of the wildlife sanctuary that was next to the B&B.

Quite a culture shock from her former skyscraper window's view that wouldn't let her see past the next building. She'd missed small-town living while working in Chicago, yet she had loved her time in the city too.

Of course, meeting Chance Garrison had also been a perk. "Argh! Why can't I stop thinking about him?"

Midnight lifted his head and looked playfully all of a sudden toward the door. "No, boy, he's not coming over again today." Midnight sighed and set his head down.

Chloe knew the feeling.

"Lord, if You think my program will benefit this town that Mom and I have already come to love, help me find a way to make this work."

Chloe might not go to church, but she knew where her drive, talent and strength came from. She also knew it was given to her for the benefit of helping others. She'd use it to the best of her ability.

Pen reunited with paper, Chloe jotted notes from her Chicago team that would benefit building an identical Refuge team—assuming the city council approved her plan.

"Ugh." Chloe set the notebook down and rubbed a hand along her face. Once she moved herself to Refuge, she'd need to replace herself on the Chicago team.

"Time for a switcheroo." Chloe fed Midnight, then opened the Chicago team's financial books. She needed more funding to get the Refuge clinic off the ground. Time for more grant writing, her least favorite chore.

Chloe pulled the ponytail holder out and pressed fingertips to her temples.

A knock sounded at her door. She grabbed some ibuprofen to fight her growing headache on the way to answer it.

When she opened it, Mandy, Celia and Amber stood grinning like cats with canary feathers springing from their mouths. "Hi!" they said in unison.

"Hi." Chloe moved aside, glad for the distraction but suspicious of the smirking faces.

Clearly, they were up to something.

"Have a seat. Rescue me from paperwork."

Rather than enter, Celia burst in and dragged Chloe toward the door. "Nope, *chica.* You're coming with us."

"Wait—what?" Chloe dug her heels into the floor. "I don't want to leave Midnight alone and—"

Amber snatched the leash and headed toward the dog. "Got him. He's coming with."

With Celia still dragging her out the door, Chloe twisted toward Mandy. "Um, where are they taking me?"

Mandy tugged her elbow. "We are friend-napping you."

They stepped outside in a giggling drove. Two more women waited in a Hummer. "Manny bought it for Celia. Isn't it gorgeous?" Amber helped Midnight into the back.

"Yes, it's to die for. Now, where are we going?"

Chloe couldn't help but laugh at the gaggle of women shoving her into Celia's new ride.

A platinum-blonde woman reached out her hand. "Hi, I'm Sarah Petrowski. We're taking you to breakfast."

"Then to show you the greatest places to shop in Refuge," Amelia Dillinger said.

Chloe smiled. "I remember you from the other night."

"Yes, and by the way, Miss Maple is a Mister."

Chloe giggled. "Does Chance know yet?"

"Ben figured he'd let Reece inform him of that."

The women chuckled together. It felt good to be surrounded by new friends. "Thank you all. Seriously, I so needed this friendly invasion."

"Sure. And later this afternoon, we're taking you to a PJ cookout." Amber clicked her seat belt.

Celia wiggled her brows. "Where Chance will be."

An older woman added, "As will you. Hi, my name's Mina."

"You look like the sensible one of the bunch." Chloe latched her seat belt and felt a sense of adventure rise. "Please tell me you're not part of the cupid posse that I see has multiplied from three women to five."

"Six," Mina said, then snickered behind her hand.

Mandy grinned. "Mina's the mastermind behind it all."

Chloe should protest. She really should.

She should demand they turn this car around and take her back instead of help run her heart and dreams into trouble over a man who was the very reason she couldn't concentrate on work today.

Instead she found herself sitting back, laughing and enjoying the ride.

Chapter Eight

Saturday morning Brock ran with Chance to St. Louis in Manny's truck to bring more of Ivan's furniture to Refuge.

"Dude, I'm hungry. Can we stop and eat?" Brock asked on the way back. He plucked sunglasses from the dash as they entered Refuge.

They'd skipped lunch to get more things packed, and Chance's stomach was protesting too. "We'll have to hit a drive-through. I left the nurse with Dad but her shift is almost over so we'll need to drop by there until Ben, Amelia and Reece show up."

"They're watching Ivan today? That's cool."

"Yeah, they offered. And the nurse came in early so we could leave sooner this morning. Ben and Amelia invited me to the PJ cookout and offered to watch Ivan since I haven't gone in a while. But I feel guilty about them missing the cookout and for leaving Dad, who feels like a burden."

For some reason, Brock stayed silent and smiled.

They purchased lunch and arrived at Ivan's. The home health nurse handed Chance her paperwork. "Not much has changed. His blood pressure is better today but still on the high side of normal." She eyed the four fast-food bags, which contained salads. "He's already had lunch and is napping."

"Thanks for making him lunch and coming in early."

"Sure. See you Tuesday." She pocketed her stethoscope.

Chance extended a salad sack. "We brought you one."

Her cheeks tinged. "How thoughtful. Thanks." She took the bag, waved and left.

Brock chuckled. "She's shy, like you."

They unloaded furniture then came inside to eat.

"Dude, I know you're a man of few words, but not with me," Brock said. "You've been unusually quiet since nurse-lady left."

Salad in hand, Chance released a long breath and sat. "High blood pressure can lead to another stroke."

"If Ivan's doc is concerned, he'll increase his meds." Brock crammed forkfuls of salad in his mouth.

"Then he won't have energy to do his therapy." Chance stared at his food. His appetite fled. He fought the despair that dogged him over Dad's tumbling health.

"Dude, you need to eat. You're losing too much weight." Brock jabbed a fork toward Chance's salad.

"Stress." Chance forced food down his throat,

but the romaine lettuce he normally loved went down like leather.

A vehicle pulled up outside. Probably Ben and Amelia. Chance didn't look. "I wonder if they brought Reece. She's good for Dad."

"She has a birthday coming up." Brock made no movement to go to the door. Chance didn't either, figuring it must have been a neighbor arriving instead of Ben and Amelia, because they would have walked right in.

"She's gonna be seven, I think." Chance chuckled. "She told Dad to get better soon so she can beat him at chess."

Brock laughed. "She probably could."

"Yeah." Chance forced another bite down then shoved the salad at Brock. "Here. I'm done."

Brock normally would have scarfed up Chance's leftovers. But he shoved the salad back. "No way. Eat."

Chance managed a few more bites. "I miss Mom's cooking on weekends." The salad turned sour in his stomach. "Today is, would have been, her and Dad's anniversary."

"I know." Brock poked around Chance's salad for grilled chicken remnants, then put Ivan's salad in the refrigerator.

Silence reigned over the room for several moments.

"I'm surprised Chloe didn't call yet today to check on Ivan." Brock pulled the blinds open to peer out the window.

"She's probably catching up from being in Chicago. She had to get some work done, she said."

"Well?" Brock stepped across the high watermelon-colored-carpet and fisted his keys.

"Well, what?"

"How're things going? You two looked pretty interested in each other at dinner last night." Brock looked out the window again, then turned and lowered himself to the sofa. Thunder clouds roiled in and started spitting serious rain. "She's single. You're single…"

Chance went to shut the blind Brock left open and paused. What was the white van in his driveway, and where was Manny's truck parked there a moment ago? "Bro, someone stole Pena's car."

Brock snickered. "Nah, he let a friend borrow it. They dropped off the van."

"So you're driving the ugly utility van and expecting to pick up chicks?" Chance laughed.

Brock shook his head and ignored the question. "Back to Chloe. I saw Mandy at the DZ after I left your place the other day. She gave me the scoop."

Chance leaned against the dresser they had yet to move into Ivan's bedroom. "If you're so interested, why don't *you* get her number?" If Brock called her, Chance might have to break his fingers.

"She wasn't making eyes at me last night. Besides, I like strawberry blondes."

Chance laughed, thinking he wouldn't tell Brock that Chloe's hair smelled like strawberries. "She wasn't making eyes." Crazy he'd even suggest so.

Last thing he needed was another distraction from work. Right? "Was she really making eyes at me?"

"Dude, maybe not intentionally, but yeah. There was definite interest brewing that very first day before she caught herself and snapped back into professional mode. You caught her off guard. No doubt."

So the powerful, unexpected attraction had been mutual from the get-go, according to Brock. "You think?"

"Absolutely. And you two hit it off at the movies. Her pupils totally dilated on you."

"Nah, it was the light."

"From her blinding smile? The one that got you so goofed up you lost your manners and made her stand on the steps for like two whole minutes when she got here that first day?"

Chance laughed. "I was trying to decide if I should let that dogzilla of hers in the door. Fine. Okay, I admit she was prettier than I expected. The kind of pretty that turns heads." The kind of pretty that could pose too big a distraction. "I barely have mental and emotional energy for everything as it is. Not that I mind taking care of Dad."

"But caregiving would be easier if your dad minded…in every sense of the word." Brock chuckled.

Chance eyed the window. "Seriously, where's Manny's truck?"

"So I hear Miss Maple ended up being a Mister."

"Stop changing the subject, but yeah, Ben had Reece inform me of that. She wants to be a vet when she grows up."

"She could. Kid's sharp as a tack."

Chance folded one ankle over the other and flipped a blind panel up again. Streaks of light beamed in. "What's really up with the van? 'Cause I'm not buying your smack story."

Brock shifted on the couch. "Just tell Ivan I instigated everything."

Chance unfolded his ankles and twisted to stare at his friend. "What are you up to?"

Brock grinned. "You'll see when the guys get here."

"The guys? Is everyone coming over or something?"

Brock shrugged and spun his keys on his pointer finger, then started whistling as he rose from the couch.

Seconds later, teammate Vince Reardon's custombuilt motorcycle rumbled into his yard. Joel's Expedition pulled in beside it. Chance watched the guys exit. A strange feeling swept through him. Had they not been smiling, he'd think this was a PJ meeting. "Am I getting kicked off the team or what?"

Brock snickered. "I couldn't be so lucky. C'mon." They opened the door and stood on the landing wet from rain.

"Dude, can I put my bike in your garage?" Vince peeled off his helmet.

"No problem." Chance stepped inside and grabbed the garage door opener.

His teammates and team leader filed into the home he would share with his dad for who knew how long.

"Hey, what's up?" Chance said to Joel, who walked over and lifted Ivan's medical bag from the floor.

Joel attached the bag to Ivan's wheelchair. "We're kidnapping you and your dad. You've been too isolated, bud. I'm ordering you to come hang with us at the PJ cookout."

"Ordering me to the cookout. Can you do that?"

Joel grinned. "Petrowski says I can."

"And just how do you think you'll get Dad there?" Chance followed Joel toward Ivan's room.

Joel shrugged. "It's not like he can outrun us or fight off five combat soldiers who are toting him to the car."

"True." Chance laughed. "This is crazy, you guys."

"We miss you, man." Manny clapped a hand on Chance's shoulder.

A freight train of emotions deposited a lump in his throat. "I don't know what to say." He'd missed getting together with them on weekends, but hadn't been able to since Mom's illness and death, then Dad's stroke had upended his life.

His entire team undoubtedly remembered this was Chance's parents' anniversary and had taken time to plan this outing for Ivan's sake. The last thing the old man needed was to sit home moping about everything he'd lost.

Brock knocked on Ivan's door, then stepped in, followed by Joel. After significant grumbling and what sounded like a minor scuffle, Ivan apparently conceded because when Joel wrestled the chair back out, a scowling Ivan was in it.

A triumphant Joel grinned behind him. Brock too.

Ivan glowered at Chance, who stuck his hands out. "Whoa now, Dad. I had nothing to do with this."

Ivan grunted and looked away. But Chance didn't miss the tears gathering in his eyes. Like Chance, he knew these rough-and-tumble men were total softies on the inside. They shared an unbreakable brotherhood and left no man behind.

Not on the field, not in life.

Ivan's tears meant he was touched by this abduction of mercy. "If you're forcing me to go, then get my bag!"

"Already got it, sir." Joel lifted the strap.

Chance didn't expect his dad to be still about it, but an unexpected smile broke over Ivan's face. It magnified as Joel and Brock struggled to push the clunky chair over the high carpet. Chance needed to rip it out and put tile or something more suitable in. But he'd hoped Dad wouldn't need the chair permanently. He refused to rethink it right now.

"What's this charade all about anyhow?" Ivan bellowed.

Joel leaned in and whispered something to Ivan, then aimed a thumb at Chance.

Ivan grinned and mumbled something to Brock that made him laugh. Everyone faced Chance. Ivan grinned wider.

"What's so funny, old man?" Chance grinned back at his dad. Good to see him having fun like this again.

"Maybe they're creating a conspiracy to help those little grandbabies along." Ivan's eyes twinkled.

Chance's smile faded and he paused midstep. "Huh?"

Ivan's grin exploded. Chance's team looked stricken with a guilt plague all of a sudden. All of them.

"What's he mean?" Chance blocked the path of all.

Vince smirked. Joel shrugged, and Ben bit his lip.

Brock's ears turned red. "Chloe's sort of coming to the cookout. Ivan says she'd make pretty babies."

"And Brock thinks she'd make you a good wife." Ivan hissed out a laugh. Good to hear it, although he hated being the brunt of the joke. "Come on, guys, lighten up on the matchmaking. Give the girl a chance to settle in first."

"So you're not opposed to dating her?" Brock asked.

Chance snorted. "You kidding me, man? Bring it!"

Ivan's eyes still twinkled when Joel loaded him into the rented van. That his team went to this much trouble to get them out of the house on what would have been a dreadful day meant more than he could articulate at the moment.

Chance swallowed and clapped a hand on Brock's back as he eyed the others. "Thanks, man. Thanks to all of you."

They nodded.

Brock eyed Chance, not with sympathy but respect. "You've been through a lot. Isolation doesn't help. Sunshine, laughter and a little socializing will do wonders."

Speaking of sunshine, Chloe's face rather than the sun came to mind.

"Shotgun," Chance called and climbed into Joel's passenger seat. "How'd you come about inviting her?"

Joel pulled onto the road. "The girls went over there with the welcoming committee. You know Celia and Amber."

"Yeah. They jump at the chance to accost any newcomer to Refuge and invite them to gatherings." Which reminded Chance that Dad's shy new nurse was also new to Refuge. He needed to let the committee know so they could extend their welcome to her.

"And you know Sarah and Amelia." Joel upped the AC.

"They can't stand to see anyone left out."

"Mina masterminded and Mandy was all over it. Val's out of town with Vince's sister at a bike show or she'd have been in the thick of it too. Mandy set it up."

"Ah. Chloe's mom, Mary, works part-time for her at the doctor's office next to the hospital." Chance slanted the vent. Cool air fanned his face. It was hot today. Nice outside.

"I'm pretty sure Mandy invited Mary too. But she took a rain check. Something about having to hang at home because the company she gets greenhouse supplies from was delivering things throughout the day," Joel said.

Chance eyed his dad when he and Brock passed

in the utility van. "Thanks, Joel. Dad looks happier than I've seen him in weeks."

"No sweat. So, tell me about this Chloe girl."

Chance blushed. "Not much to tell."

Joel grinned. "Not yet."

"Not yet, but thanks," Chloe said to the sweet blond-headed boy named Bradley who held a tray of Mountain Dew Apple Dumplings up to her nose. As tempting as those sweet-smelling treats were, she first wanted the meat and corn grilling on the patio, courtesy of PJ commander Petrowski.

"Sarah, your yard is gorgeous." Chloe looked around at the beauty of vibrant flowers, edging and shrubs.

Aaron pulled his bride close and kissed her temple. "I owe most of it to her."

"I had help from my dual little landscapers." Sarah smiled at five-year-old twins, playing with Reece in the yard. Midnight romped in the thick circle of squealing, leaping fun, as did two dogs named Shasta and Mooch, whom Midnight instantly bonded to.

Sarah cleared her throat. "So, there's a romantic tradition at the PJ cookouts."

Romantic? Chloe eyed her suspiciously. "Yeah? What's that?"

"Couples, married, dating or otherwise interested in each other, go for a little hike while the older women, like Mina, watch the kiddos."

"Oh, that's nice. And your point is?" Chloe hid her grin behind her water bottle. She sipped the last drop.

Southern Illinois was so humid she never felt dry enough on the outside or hydrated enough on the inside.

"Just letting you know. In case…" Sarah smiled.

Despite the water, Chloe's mouth dried. "In case what?" If Sarah was hinting at Chloe helping Mina with the kids, she was all for it. She loved children. She just didn't want her own yet. She needed to build her program first so she could focus on her children fully when the time came.

A bunch of cars pulled up the Petrowskis' picturesque drive. Her pulse took on a frenetic pace when Chance slid from a white SUV like a knight in camouflage armor.

His words from their dinner at the restaurant drifted through her mind. He'd made no secret that he wanted children young. *You'll make a wonderful father to your children…and a great husband to some lucky lady someday.* Regret poked holes in her resolve. Mental patches didn't help. He looked *so* cute walking and talking, expressing and gesturing and—

"Chloe?"

Chloe removed her hand from patting her hair and faced Sarah. "Yes?" She blinked.

Sarah peered at Chance, now helping his dad from an industrial van. "Oh. Now I see why you didn't hear my question." She giggled.

Chloe's face heated. "I, well, er, sorry, what were you asking?"

Sarah's grin widened. "I asked three times if you'd met anyone interesting since staying in Refuge."

"But we can clearly see now that you have." Celia flailed arms toward Chance and danced like a penguin.

Mandy winked at Amelia. Mina snickered. Then Amber joined in.

Chloe kicked multiple shins under the picnic table. "You're all as bad as my cousin Mallory. Shh! Here he comes. And for the record, I'm not taking that walk."

"I wonder if he's just as interested." Mandy sipped a bottle of water and eyed Chance.

Just then his face lifted, and he caught sight of Chloe. His steps faltered and his grin exploded. He waved, then blushed when the surrounding PJs socked his arm.

Mina snorted into her hand. "Well. No question there."

Chloe bit her lip to keep from smiling. "Seriously, guys. Don't push. Things would never work between us."

But rather than heed her appeal for a cease-fire on the cupid posse arrows, the women fell into peals of laughter.

"What?" Chloe blinked.

"That's exactly what every one of us said about our PJs too and look what happened." Sarah brandished a diamond ring and her wedding band. The other four women followed suit by lifting their sparkly, adorned left hands.

"And Vince's wife, Val, would say the same if she were here," Amelia said.

Amber nodded. "She never thought things would work out between her and Vince."

"I'm not taking the walk." Their dinner and movie had been a friendship outing, right?

Snorting, Mina scooted over, presumably to leave a place next to her since Chance had settled his dad under a shady spot and was jogging over.

Everything in Chloe wanted to protest. But the words died as Chance drew near.

"Hey, Chloe." His voice melted over her like sweet liquid chocolate on a fondue fountain. How could it catch her so off guard?

And how could she forget every single time just how deep and dreamy and pleasant to the ears his voice was?

And why did it resonate straight through to her soul?

The women, still laughing, dispersed.

"Wow. Like that's not obvious," Chloe muttered, fisting her lid and snapping the top off her bottle. "I see Ivan's here. That's wonderful!"

He smiled at his dad. "Yeah. Today would have been his and Mom's anniversary. Manny and Celia were both widowed before meeting each other. They say the first year of all the 'firsts' without their loved one is hardest. I think that's why everyone arranged this."

Thick emotion in Chance's throat when he spoke yanked her heart to attention. Her world fell by the wayside and her mind orbited into a daze as he turned, bent and extended his hand and an irresistible smile.

"So, there's a bunch of squirrels in the woods that I have nearly tamed. Want to walk with me and see 'em?"

"Walk?" she squeaked.

"Yeah, and there's a family of deer with twin spotted fawns in a field near the squirrels. We'll take carrots. They'll come right up and eat out of our hands."

Like he had her eating out of his right now with his contagious exuberance over the animals.

"And I rescued a beaver from a tangle of barbed wire down the end of a stream. He'll sometimes come up and let me toss him crackers. He's cute."

So are you. Wait, rescued? "You *rescued* a beaver? A live, wild one?"

He nodded. Eyes scanned the crowds of people conglomerating in various parts of the yard. Some couples started down the trail of doom, which disgustingly now half appealed, half repelled.

Chance refastened his gaze on hers and drifted closer. "You're the only one here who totally gets me and my concern for these animals. I'd love nothing more than to share them with you. It'd mean a lot to me if you'd walk the hike with me."

This man's life had been bereft of joy for six solid months. He'd weathered loss like a five-star soldier.

How could she consider denying him this one small pleasure? An inner flush crept from her stomach to her chest.

"I...uh...mmm...not sure that—"

He smiled. "Please? For me?" And as if that wasn't

convincing enough, he wove his arm through hers and slid his strong, warm hand agonizingly slowly down her inner forearm until their hands nestled palm to palm.

His touch, both sure and pure, seared her flesh with fires of innocence that branded in her a deep and irrefutable knowing.

This is your soul mate. This is meant to be.

Awestruck, her heart and hope leaped inside her.

The world around the two of them faded away. All the personal protests and reasons she shouldn't ceased to exist in her mind. The chaos calmed.

All she could see was Chance.

And every reason she wanted to go.

Chance's alluring eyes and softened face hitched her breath and sent her pulse skittering because he had the look of a man falling in love. He gently drew her close and tugged her up. "Walk with me, Chloe?"

Gazes welded, she rose—a little dazed, a little dreamy—and definitely not caring that every surprised woman in the cupid posse probably gawked and cheered and that she'd have to eat crow later.

She wanted nothing more this moment than to take that walk with Chance.

And two hours later she wanted to take the walk with him again and again and again. When they returned to the yard, Ivan's face brightened as he observed them approach hand-in-hand. Chance grinned down at her and squeezed.

"See coons and squirrels?" Ivan asked Chloe. His eyes twinkled.

She eyed Chance and respect rose for him as did admiration. "I did." She'd also seen inside the heart of a man who loved animals as much as she. A heart she could lose herself loving.

Chance released her hand but let his fingers brush hers in the process. "Looks like the party's wrapping up. You ready to leave Dad?"

Ivan's smile faded. "I reckon if I have to." His eyes said otherwise. Chloe could relate. She didn't want this day, or their walk to ever end. She smiled at Ivan and studied Chance. "Maybe we could make this an every-Saturday outing?" Excitement welled up when twin grins erupted on the Garrison men's faces, flooding her with equal hope and fear.

Chapter Nine

Chance whistled long and low as he knelt to view the wicked rash covering Chloe's shins four weeks later when she arrived for Ivan's thrice-weekly therapy.

Mondays, Wednesdays and Fridays had grown to be Chance's favorite three days of the week the past month. But Saturdays beat all.

The more he'd gotten to know Chloe, the more he wanted to know more. He called every morning to wish her a good day and every evening to say sweet dreams. They'd rescued and placed animals in homes together. One rescue involved a neglected puppy, whom they placed with a foster child who'd suffered the same. Every incident sealed in his mind the importance of Chloe's program, and her growing importance to him. Their bond deepened more with every passing Saturday, especially during their walks at the past few PJ cookouts. Ivan's mood and health had improved as well. Getting out had done wonders for the both of them.

"Are you sure it's some kind of plant poison?" Chloe nibbled her lip and wiggled her knees together, probably to ease the itch. "I don't recall us hiking through nettles or any three-leafed plants at the last PJ cookout."

"No, but Midnight did. And I'm sure you've petted him since the last hike." Chance rose and went to his bathroom medicine cabinet.

Chloe followed, her body twitching and contorting like a spastic windup toy. "What do you think it is?"

"Could be poison parsnip, but most likely it's just a bad case of poison ivy."

"How long will that last?"

"About two, three weeks…if you don't scratch." He intercepted her hand, which looked about to do just that. "When and how'd it start?"

"I noticed at bedtime last night that I had a slight spot on my knee. Then I woke up in the middle of the night to positively the itchiest experience in my life. I don't deal well with itching."

Chance nodded and opened a bottle of calamine lotion.

"I turned on the light and saw this strand of blisters but thought I was just having an allergic reaction to something I ate day before yesterday at the cookout. Did I mention itching drives me berserk?" She jabbed her hand toward her shin.

Chance was faster. Hand there, he pressed it over hers before her fingernails could make their mark.

She stuck her tongue at him and tried to wriggle her hand free.

"Sit on them. That'll help."

Surprisingly, she complied.

"I took Benadryl. It made me sleep late. I went to the Refuge City Council meeting groggy and felt unprepared. Steele and Bunyan aren't budging. I'm trying to get a majority vote, but Bunyan insists I need unanimous for clearance."

"Let me know how to help you, Chloe, and I will."

She blinked and seemed surprised at that. Doubtful, even, that he was sincere. One day, the girl would learn he wasn't like her dad. He would be there. He needed to be patient and not push, or like the wounded forest animals he was in the habit of helping, she'd run scared.

He rubbed a calamine-soaked cotton ball over her rash to ease the itch. "What else?"

"Each time I woke up, the rash and horrible itching had spread. Then this morning my shins and ankles were covered in these gigantic red sores. And outlandish itching. Like, the intense, relentless kind that could seriously drive a person insane."

He chuckled. "Welcome to southern Illinois, Chloe."

She smacked his arm, then eyed the room where Ivan was napping. "Is this contagious? Should we reschedule? I hate to share my 'goodies' with you or Ivan. Well, Ivan," she smirked, "since you won't let me scratch."

Chance laughed and stood. "I've never reacted to poison ivy, but there's always a first. It shouldn't be contagious."

He handed her the phone. "Call Mandy. She and Nolan are on speed dial three. Have her phone you in a script at the local drugstore, and I'll go pick it up."

Her eyes brightened. It stole his breath when she looked at him like her hero. "Will it stop the itching?"

"You bet. And you should be fine to do Dad's therapy, if you can keep from scratching."

"Well, to keep from scratching I need to keep from itching. I have zero self-control when it comes to not scratching itches. Will the rash spread if I accidentally scratch?" Her fingers inched toward her knees.

His hand covered hers. He didn't want to release it. He hated that she suffered from poison ivy but loved that the wicked itch gave him a worthy excuse to hold her hand. "Probably not, but you could get a secondary infection."

She clicked her tongue. "This is all your fault, you know. You and that rabid beaver."

"He's not rabid. That shriek you let out scared him."

"Well, I didn't expect him to get so close. Beavers can be mean, you know." Her other hand snaked down to her ankle.

His free hand covered hers, halting it. "Beavers? Nothing like the coon you tried to approach." He winked.

"But it was cute." She rubbed her ankles together and flopped her feet on the floor. Chance tried not to laugh.

"Next to badgers and possums when they're not

playing dead, coons are the most vicious animals in that forest."

"How can something that innocent looking be mean?"

"That's what most people say about poison ivy after they've had a run-in with it." Chuckling, Chance went to wake Ivan so Chloe could expedite her therapy.

When he came out of his room, Ivan's head swerved left and right, and his eyes scoured to and fro. Then his countenance tanked. "Where's the goofy mutt?"

"I left him home. Chance thinks he has urushiol oil on his hair." Chloe pulled out the hand wheel machine.

"U-roo-what?" Ivan's face squished.

Chance pointed to Chloe's ankles. "Poison ivy."

"Oh. Gotcha." Ivan rubbed a hand over his chin. His affected hand, Chance noticed. *Hoo-rah!*

"Shall we get started?" Chloe faced Ivan.

"I reckon." Ivan took on the scowl he always adopted before therapy. Only today's seemed genuine. As though he really was disappointed not to get to see "the mutt."

"You know, if you get your arms to the point of using a walker, then a cane, you could take Midnight for strolls." Chloe secured his affected hand to the pedaled structure.

Her words sparked something in Ivan, because determination Chance hadn't witnessed since the stroke suddenly flashed across his face. His eyes scanned the empty hook where Chloe always hung Midnight's leash and walking harness. The wheel turned smoother and faster than before.

Chance slipped out, thankful even more for Chloe, her unconventional ways and handy-dandy assistant who'd obviously barked his way into Ivan's joy-parched heart.

And gifted Chloe with poison ivy and given Chance a reason to hold her hand when she couldn't resist itching.

"So, Dad, I'm getting the fishing boat from your garage this week. How about we go to Refuge Lake this weekend?" Chance asked when he returned with Chloe's poison ivy meds.

"Are you nuts? I can't do that. You're a fool for thinking it." Ivan's scowl set firmly in place.

Chloe put Ivan's chart away. "I saw your Web site, the one where you have your custom-built chess sets for sale."

His face lit, then took a nose dive. "Oh, you did?"

"Yes. Mighty fine craftsmanship."

"Too bad I can't do it anymore."

"I think you can. Keep up the good work and do your exercises, and you'll be making chess sets again in no time."

"Hmph. You're as foolish as my son there. I'll never be what I was. Not without my wife."

Chloe's expression grew thoughtful. She turned to Chance while Ivan stretched his isometric therapy band. "I noticed fishing photos of you." For some odd reason her cheeks tinged and she scratched the side of her neck.

Chance eyed there, prepared to pull her hand down if he saw blisters, but her skin was silky and alabaster and so soft looking he wished he could brush fingers along it.

Chance cleared his throat. "Uh, yeah? Why?"

"Mom and I used to fish all the time. We've heard there are huge bass and catfish in these parts." Her eyes gave off several enormous blinks, waiting for him to get the hint.

Chance grinned. "If I didn't know any better, Miss Chloe Callett, I'd think you were asking me out on a date."

Ivan must've been eavesdropping because he snorted.

She pinked. "Not a date. A fishing excursion. With Mom."

Chance displayed his lopsided grin. "Whatever works. As long as I get to stare into your lovely eyes and listen to your beautiful laugh, I'm there."

He thought her laugh was beautiful and eyes lovely? Maybe he was just being nice or joking. Chloe studied him. His smile never faded nor did the intent look of tenderness.

A knot formed in her stomach, then moved to her chest and throat. Chance had made no secret of the fact that he was on the hunt for a wife. He wasn't the type to date someone he wouldn't consider marrying. Should she date him?

While they were far from serious, definite interest did exist. But the last thing she could give Chance Garrison was forever or even a hint of the promise of it.

Not with her. They had different dreams, different priorities.

She put her hand on his arm and felt like she could cry. She urged him into the kitchen and away from Ivan's miracle hearing aids. "Chance, I'd love to go fishing with you…as friends."

Instead of acting wounded, he flashed his trademark lopsided grin again. "That's all you can muster for now?"

"That's all I can muster…forever."

His face grew neutral while he studied her intently and for so long she couldn't stand it.

Since she had grown up under the punishment of silent treatments from her dad, silence made her anxious. "What? Why are you looking at me like that?"

He took methodical steps closer. Trailed a finger along her neck and tilted her chin up. There was absolutely nothing shy about the way he looked at her. "Chloe, don't ask me that question unless you really want to know the answer." Fierce warning flashed in his tender eyes as they dropped to her mouth and appeared to outline her lips.

The way his gaze dipped, she knew he would have kissed her unconscious had Ivan not been in the next room.

She also knew she would have let him.

Until things she'd dreamed of doing since childhood tore through her mind.

"I need to know, Chance, how you feel about me. About us. Because I have plans in life that can't be broken. Not by anyone."

He nodded. "Fair enough. I have dreams too. But who's to say our dreams can't meld? The only thing I'm going to say is that you and me, we're about partnership, Chloe. Teamwork. That's how I operate. That's how it'd be. Whether we're friends or more. For the record, I hope it's more."

Again, nothing shy about his words.

"Your job is important. More important than mine. You rescue people. I rescue animals."

"No, Chloe. We both rescue people. There's no difference in me hauling stranded hikers off Mount Hood and you saving that battered dog and giving his life meaning by loving and teaching him to pluck Dad from a depression so deep I couldn't reach him anymore."

How did Chance know about Midnight's horrible past?

And how many other at-risk animals and people needed her help and wouldn't be helped if she quit the program in order to please herself?

Tears flooded Chloe's eyes. "I can't sacrifice my childhood dreams for a new one. Do you understand?"

His face softened. "I understand that God can show you He loves you any way He wants."

"What's that supposed to mean?" It came out desperate, but she truly wanted to know. When Chance spoke, she knew he'd grasped a God-truth she needed.

He'd learned God through his trials. Experienced Him and His love. Chloe sensed from the quiet confidence in his words that he'd come out on the other side of suffering with the treasure of knowing God better.

"There are things in your future that you can't begin to imagine, Chloe. Things you want that are buried so deep inside you, desires and hopes you aren't even vaguely aware of." Cupping her face, he smiled tenderly, and both his look and his touch held a promise she was terrified to grasp. "Yet."

She swallowed and took a step back, her mother's warning dogging her. Words she'd heard since childhood.

Don't let any man get in the way of what you want.

"Not only that, Chance, you are going to end up a pastor someday, the one kind of person I promised myself never to marry."

"You made that vow out of brokenness because of your dad." His jaw hardened, yet his eyes yielded to an empathetic softness. "I'm not your dad."

She shook her head. More to clear the cobwebs than because she wanted to ponder his words. "I know what I want, and this doesn't fit."

Now he looked like he could laugh. "Of course not. Our dreams rarely do. But God knows how to fish, Chloe. To draw deep things out of us. Especially when He planted seeds there in the first place. I pray He does it sooner rather than later. I want a family while I'm young. I know we'd be good together."

"You're saying you won't wait for me forever."

That should have made her feel relieved. Instead it made her feel like rushing to the restroom and throwing up.

Especially when his answer was silence. Not a stormy kind of dark and brooding silence. Nor dead-fish cold and punishing like her dad's used to be when he was alive.

But a quiet, confident, resolutely sad kind of silence. And it spoke volumes to her heart and mind.

This man wanted a future. He wanted it with her.

But if she didn't want it back, he didn't plan to wait around for her to get it. And no woman in her right mind would turn down this astronomically appealing man who possessed high-caliber character. Was she out of her mind?

Feeling suddenly on the brink of a place she promised herself she would never go, Chloe scrambled for something. Anything to repel him and break this spellbinding connection.

"Really? God has good things for us? You can say this after you lost your mother and almost lost your father?"

The jolted look on his face resembled the slap of remorse instantly jabbing through her like a sharp arrow.

She gasped. "I'm so sorry, Chance. I don't know why I said something so cruel." *What on earth was wrong with her?*

She expected harsh words, then the dreaded lash of silence. Instead, an undeserved look of understanding graced his face. "Maybe because of fear over the feelings you and I both know are forming between us."

She swallowed, feeling weirdly exposed, yet

compelled with the need to apologize. "Forgive me." She gulped.

"I know you're not prone to making insensitive comments, so I'll chalk it up to lack of sleep last night because of the poison ivy. And for the record, I'll wait as long as I can without jeopardizing quality time with my children and grandchildren."

Chloe blinked. Obviously by that comment, he was willing to wait awhile. She clutched her collar to her throat and grabbed her bag. "I need to go. I'll tell Ivan goodbye."

He nodded and followed her from the kitchen but didn't walk her to her car today like normal. She missed his presence more than she expected to. She'd taken his friendship for granted.

Dogged by regret and other things she didn't dare try to decipher, Chloe threw herself into her SUV. "All I have to say, Miss G, is that once I attain my dream, it had better be worth it. Especially considering what I have to leave behind in order to see it come to pass."

Feeling Chance's eyes on her, she turned to face the house.

He stood on the landing, hands braced casually on the porch molding above. He looked like a muscle-clad letter *X*.

She swallowed and looked away. Started her car.

He stepped off the porch.

Her heart leapt. She should drive away. Now. She forced her fingers to put the car in drive and inched from the curb.

"Chloe, wait!" His feet thundered across the yard and down the sidewalk. She applied the brakes and rolled her driver's side window down, then blinked back tears at the tortured look on his face.

In a storm of movement, he bent all the way into her window, hands reaching for her. Never breaking eye contact, he swaddled the sides of her face tenderly. Firmly. Carefully. Sure.

And promptly kissed her.

For who knew how long, because her body sank until it melted into her leather seats.

Her car started rolling. Chance jerked back to prevent being dragged by the car and bumped his head in the process. She jammed her foot on the brake and slammed the gear in park. "Sorry. Didn't realize I left it in drive."

He rubbed his head and slowly unfurled that hallmark lopsided grin. Her face flushed. Whether from the delicious kiss or the fact that she nearly ran over the handsome one issuing it, she wasn't sure. Nor was she sure how such a shy guy learned to smooch like *that*.

But she was sure of one thing. Her heart was in serious jeopardy.

Which meant her unmet dreams were sure to follow?

Chance reached in and grasped her hands, wringing themselves in her lap. "Give me hope, Chloe. One sliver is all I need." His eyes held irresistible appeal. "Promise you'll at least pray about it? Please," he whispered.

Though it could have been construed by someone who didn't know him better as begging, this man was far from desperate.

This was the appeal of a quietly confident man falling fiercely in love and unwilling to walk away from what he wanted without a worthy fight.

Her chest fluttered at the thought and the new, unexpected possibilities. Sharp, achy urges to cling to his stalwart promise thrummed through her. Her heart pulsed with want she didn't know it possessed. It longed to let the care bloom in her for him too, to let it plume open in the light of his growing affection. Together, they could nourish their feelings to grow until they reached the whispered edges of forever.

Staring into his soulful eyes, how badly she wanted to cave. How badly that scared her.

But the anchor of her dreams dragged heavily. They'd been there longer, were stronger.

She knew what she must do.

Pain streaked through her. She'd never felt so morbidly sad. Not since losing her dad and along with him, the hope that they'd ever be close.

She squeezed Chance's hand, brought it to her mouth, and planted a final kiss. Then she raised her own hand to wipe an unbidden tear streaking down her face.

"I'm sorry, Chance. Unlike my dad, I can't promise something that's never going to happen."

Chapter Ten

❧

"**W**hat's wrong with you, boy? You haven't moped like this since you ran your Honda 50 into the eight-foot-deep hole the neighbor dug for his septic tank."

Chance chuckled grimly at the memory. "Yeah, the way I remember that is you wouldn't help me out. You stood on the edge and said if I got myself and that bike in there, I had to get us out or I couldn't ride it anymore."

"But you got it out, didn't you?"

"After a long hour."

"Nope. It was twelve minutes 'n' forty-seven seconds. And you've no idea how long and torturous that twelve minutes was for me. I smelt gasoline leaking all over you. But if I bailed you out that time, I knew you'd try to jump that hole again and endanger yourself despite the fact that I told you to stay away from it. Am I right?"

Chance grinned. "Probably so."

"For real, what's goin' on between you and my OT?"

"Nothing."

"Which is precisely the problem."

"What makes you say that?"

"Because you've been limping around in a bad, sad mood since the day she dragged you into the kitchen. You conveniently find someplace else to be on Mondays, Wednesdays and Fridays. It just so happens you're gone during the hours she's scheduled to be here and on Saturdays too."

Chance eyed Ivan's therapy schedule on the wall. "I've been busy with PJ trainings." Partly true.

Ivan snickered. "Right. And I'm a rocket scientist."

"Given the opportunity, you could have been."

"Given the opportunity, I'd come out of this chair and turn you over my knee for treating that girl that way."

"Chloe's fine, Dad."

"Fine? Where've you been? Oh, that's right. You've been doing your best to avoid her."

"It's what she wanted."

"Then what she wanted isn't what she thought it'd be."

"Why do you say that? Seriously, Dad, don't blow smoke."

Ivan grew as serious as Chance had seen him in a while. The kind of serious that reminded Chance of former times, of life the way it once was, of a time when Ivan took care of Chance and gave him advice and guidance instead of the other way around. "Son, sit down."

Chance sat, glad to see glimpses of his old dad back.

"Though she tries her best to be professional and lighthearted, she mopes twice as bad as you do. So does that mutt. Why, he drags his tail around the house from room to room to room whining and looking for you."

Chance sat back, folding his arms across his chest.

"And when he can't find you, he circles your jump boots exactly seven times then flops down on the floor and curls his body around them. Then he whimpers to beat the band. It's the saddest, most pathetic thing I've ever seen."

"I think you're embellishing that story the same way you used to embellish those clay sets."

"Speaking of which, Chloe asked if I'd pass the message along to you to pick me up some clay. She wants me to try to start molding it as therapy."

Arms unfurled, Chance sat up. "And you're willing?"

"Of course. I'd love nothing more than to be able to work with clay again."

"And I'd love nothing more than to see you do it."

"And to see Chloe again?"

"Dad, she has other priorities. Don't meddle."

Ivan snickered. "Who, me?"

Two days later, Chloe's car pulled up exactly five minutes after Chance arrived home. Chance turned to Ivan. "I should have known. Should have suspected something amiss when you told me Chloe was coming in early today."

Ivan adopted an overly innocent look and tapped his ears, conveniently void of hearing aids. "What's that you say?"

Chance smirked and went to answer the door. "You hear me loud and clear. You set me up, Dad." Clearly, Chloe'd planned to be here at her usual time. Had Chance known that, he wouldn't have rearranged his schedule to avoid her this morning, when Ivan said she'd be there.

Which meant that his dad had officially joined the—what was it Chloe called it?—oh yeah, the cupid posse.

She stumbled at the landing when he opened the door to let her in. For a brief second, Chance thought about passing her and going right out the gate and to his Jeep.

But something in her eyes stopped him.

"Hi." She brushed a tendril of hair behind her ear.

"Hi." His mouth tightened the way it did before he stuttered so he left it at the short greeting.

He stepped aside and averted his gaze. She shouldered in, looking more beautiful than the images his mind had tormented him with the past few weeks.

Chloe set down the delicious-smelling meatloaf dinner she'd brought. "Did Ivan mention the clay?"

"It's on the table."

"Okay. Thanks." She swallowed hard and seemed distracted. Her hands quaked as she pulled stuff from her bag.

He wanted nothing more than to rush over and hold her. He took tentative steps toward her. "This is hard for me too, Chloe," he whispered once close.

She nodded. Drew in a sharp breath. "I've missed you." She blinked several times and appeared to search rapidly for something in her bag.

"Can I help you find something?" he asked.

When her face lifted, tears filled her eyes. She gulped a swallow. "Yes. I need help finding the resolve I need to be able to stay away from you. And I need to find strength not to think about you every second of the day. I need you to help me look for whatever it's going to take to erase you from my mind. And free me from the urge to drive past the DZ to catch glimpses of you," she whispered in a scratchy voice.

Joy filled him with every word spoken. He grinned. "Drive by the DZ. You do? Really?"

Her face tinged pink. "No."

He tilted his chin. "No?"

She shook her head. "But I've wanted to. Especially on Tuesdays when I know you're training recruits outside."

Without hesitation or prompting he closed the distance between them and pulled her into his arms. Held her tight.

And, thank God, she let him.

She sighed. "At first I couldn't do what you asked. Couldn't pray. But then, I don't know, God started dogging me. And He wouldn't relent. Pestered me until I prayed."

"And now?"

"I don't know, Chance. I just know I don't want to live without you, but I don't want to see my dreams die either."

"So let's take it slow. Let come what may. Let what will be, be."

"Can we start back at friendship?"

"It'll be torture not kissing you again, but I'll try. How about we go fishing this weekend? Just you and me?"

"And Mom. Because if you try to kiss me, Chance Garrison, I will surely be powerless to stop you."

The images and possibilities that provoked caused him to eye her supple mouth. She ducked under his arm and grabbed her stuff off the table. "Time for Ivan's therapy. Bring the clay. And be amazed."

His Chloe was back. The spunky, fun, witty, zesty girl he'd first met was traipsing through his kitchen right now.

He gathered the clay and followed. A sense of thankfulness washed over him. He paused and put his hand on his mother's Bible, near her cookbooks on the counter. He was so grateful to her for the example she'd set by living her faith out loud, yet quietly, day in, day out in front of him. Even though he hadn't embraced it until recently, the mortal, moral and immortal impact remained.

Whispers rose from his lips, "I don't need clay to be amazed, God. I know You're working on Chloe. Thank You. Keep molding her heart and her future and help me know how to help all she hopes for to come true. Even the dreams buried that she doesn't realize are in desperate need of rescue."

"This thing is a dream!" Mary neared the beautiful fishing boat on a trailer attached to Chance's Jeep.

"Wow." Chloe tried not to drool over the glitter-coated red-and-silver Bass Tracker. "Gorgeous."

Chance stepped from behind the trolling motor and grinned. "Yeah, it's high-end. Pretty top-of-the-line. It's also Brock's. He's coming with us. Hope you ladies don't mind. He's an avid angler. When he heard the word *fishing* he pretty much invited himself."

Mary chuckled. "He'll be in good company. Chloe and I love to fish. We don't mind Brock crashing our fishing party. Do we?"

Chloe took the heavy cooler from her mom. "Of course not. The more, the merrier. I just wish we could have talked your dad into coming," she said to Chance.

"Is he well enough to fish?" Mary transferred their fishing poles from Chloe's SUV to Chance's Jeep.

"He is, but I think he's scared he won't be up to par." Chloe slid the cooler filled with the day's nourishment inside the hatch of Chance's Jeep.

"What's his first name?"

"Chance's dad?"

Mary nodded and handed Chloe their tackle boxes. "Ivan."

Mary set her backpack inside the car. "Oh, I always did like that name."

Chloe eyed her mom, then Chance, who'd paused at that comment. A strange look crossed his face before he resumed packing the boat. "Brock ought to be here shortly."

On cue, a flashy yellow car sped around the corner and slid into the drive. Music thumped from speakers inside the sports car until the ignition shut off. Brock emerged smiling and waving at the women, then popped his trunk.

Midnight danced around Brock's ankles until he stopped what he was doing to pet the dog. "Hey, buddy."

Chloe knelt near where Chance checked taillights on the trailer. "You sure Midnight will be okay on the boat?"

"As sure as I am that you're more beautiful than that gorgeous boat." His nearness and lopsided grin as his gaze brushed her lips flushed her face. "Midnight's a web-footed, sleek-coated, water-loving dog, remember?" He winked at her then eyed the Lab, content under Brock's affection.

"Sometimes I forget. Just like you forget that this fishing trip is among *friends*."

"Spoilsport," Chance said, still grinning, and rose.

Brock approached with an arsenal of fishing lures, poles, reels and the biggest tackle box Chloe'd ever seen. "Hello, ladies." He nodded to Chloe then her mother. "You must be Mary. Mandy speaks highly of you."

Mary nodded. "Nice to meet you, Brock. You must be serious about fishing." She bug-eyed his equipment and burst out laughing. "And I thought Chloe and I were bad to drag half the shed with us when we go on a fishing trip."

Chloe stepped back so Brock could load his gear. "So, what kind of boat is that?"

Brock's eyes sparkled as he ran a hand along glitter-flaked paint. "It's a Ranger 21-footer,

250-horsepower, 24-volt, 70-pound-thrust, foot-controlled trolling motor."

Mary laughed. Chloe shook her head. "In other words, a high-end Bass Tracker."

"Is there anything else worth having?" Brock chuckled and closed the hatch to Chance's Jeep. "Shall we?"

Everyone loaded in the vehicle. It didn't escape Chloe's notice that Brock hopped in the backseat next to her mom, leaving Chloe to ride with Chance in the front.

She sighed. "Two more recruits to the cupid posse," she muttered and tugged her seat belt across her lap.

Chance covered a chuckle and started the ignition.

"Where are we fishing today, kiddos?" Mary asked as they started down the road. Chloe wondered why they hadn't used Ivan's boat today. Maybe it wasn't as big as Brock's.

"Refuge Lake, where it feeds into Refuge River, just down from Reunion Bridge," Chance said. "We ought to hit right when the fish are biting."

Two hours later, Chloe measured her tenth catch, then put the fish back in the water. She rebaited, then recast her line.

She stepped to the middle of the boat and sat next to Chance, engaged in conversation with Mary and Brock.

Chloe could hardly concentrate on what they were saying because her gaze kept tangling on Chance's myriad of facial expressions as he listened to Mary and Brock talk.

Chloe tried to force herself to tune out her un-sinkable interest in Chance and tune her mother in, but like occupied bobbers, it kept bouncing back up.

When she remembered that Chance intended to be ordained as a youth pastor, her attention finally stayed where she wanted it to.

Mary donned a visor. "Sounds like you're serious about the sport. Do you compete in tour-naments and the like?"

"Yes, ma'am. I'm not a leisurely fly fisherman like Chance here." Brock clapped a hand over his shoulder.

Oh well. Scratch introducing Brock to her cousin Mallory. She hated fishing and would have his pro-fessional fishing poles heisted and hidden within the first five minutes of meeting him.

Probably for the better anyway that Brock and Mal were polar opposites. Because if Brock was in Mallory's life, and Mallory was in Chloe's life, she'd see even more of Chance, Brock's best friend. And the more Chance became embedded in her life, the less hold she had on her heart and dreams.

For sure, her emotional fingers were slipping.

And she needed to do something about it. Fast.

Chapter Eleven

"Wow. Fast." Mary eyed the TV screen at Chance's house a few weeks after that first fishing trip. She watched intently as a line of parachutes streamed from a military craft hovering over blue water sloshed into a bowl shape by blade-blown wind.

Mary and Chloe had joined Chance and Brock on four fishing trips in the past four weeks now, and Mary had asked to see what PJs do. Chance obliged by inviting her and Chloe over to watch video footage of Petrowski's team trainings used in PJ recruiting videos.

Not that he was trying to impress Chloe or anything.

He peeked over his shoulder at her profile.

Her mouth hung open. Adoration and respect shone in her eyes as footage played of his team performing over-ocean jump exercises and deep-water rescue training for astronauts while NASA officials looked on.

She looked totally impressed. Totally immersed. Totally enthralled.

He tried to smother a grin.

Brock smirked. An *I'm-happy-for-you-but-jealous-it's-not-happening-for-me* look passed between the two men.

Chance laughed and rose to check on his dad, asleep since before they arrived. When he cracked open the door, rustling sounded. He tried to close the door quietly, hoping he hadn't disturbed his father's sleep.

"Who's there?"

Chance stepped back inside the pitch-black room. "It's me, Dad. Didn't mean to wake you."

"I've been awake. Who's out there?"

"I have some friends over. Brock and Chloe are here with her mom, Mary. We just got back from fishing."

"If Chloe's here, where's the mutt?"

Chance smiled. Even in the dark, his dad's eyes sparkled when he spoke of Midnight. "He's out there too. Sleeping at present. We wore him out fishing today. We went longer than the last two Saturdays because the fish were really biting. Wish you could have joined us."

A grunt. The bed creaked. "Reach me my clothes there."

"You're getting up?"

"Yeah. No use lying around."

Yet that's all Dad had done since the stroke.

Thankfulness washed over him because his dad was starting to feel well enough physically and emotionally to socialize. After helping his father dress, Chance pushed his wheelchair close.

Ivan growled. "Must you treat me like I can't do for myself? Hand me that cane, would ya?"

Chance grinned, loving that his dad's determination had returned in full force. At least for today.

Maybe he'd come fishing with them next weekend.

Chance flipped on the lamp. Light flooded the room. "How about use your walker first? Then graduate to cane?"

"Fine. Hold me back, why don't ya."

Chance chuckled. This was the dad he remembered.

"You say there's a lady out there?" Ivan scratched his chin and ran a hand down his trousers in smoothing motions.

Chance straightened Ivan's collar. "Yes, Chloe's mom."

"Isn't she a widow?" Ivan leaned on his walker and brushed a hand along the ring of white hair surrounding the shiny bald spot.

Chance's smile faded. "Yes, I b-believe she is."

What was up with *that?* He hadn't stuttered in days.

Mary, Chloe and Brock turned and stood when Ivan clomped into the room on his walker.

When his gaze met Mary's, a twinkle came to his eyes that made Chance uneasy. Same twinkle Chance recalled seeing once or twice when Ivan stared at Chance's mother.

"I'm Mary." She smiled and extended her hand.

"I always did like the name Mary." Ivan took her hand, then took his time releasing it.

A horrible feeling struck Chance. Surely Mary and Ivan wouldn't become interested in one another?

But the connection Chance witnessed when Mary helped his dad sit on the couch next to her nixed his hopes of zero interest. The brief but powerful thing surging between his father and Chloe's mother reminded Chance of the exact thing between himself and Chloe the first moment they met.

His gaze found Chloe's, and she too was eyeing Ivan and Mary with a curious gleam.

Unlike Chance, Chloe was smiling.

"We're watching videos," Brock said to Ivan and caught Chance's gaze in a way that let him know Brock had picked up on Chance's uncomfortable thoughts about the two parents.

Ivan pointed at a cabinet below the television. "Fetch those. That's my boy when he was learning to love airplanes. He used to build and then fly them. Thankfully for mankind he decided against being a pilot." Ivan chuckled. "And you'll soon see why."

"I d-dread this." Chance chuckled. Chloe eyed him with humor as she plucked a DVD out and poked it in.

Soon images of a teenaged Chance flying model planes came across the screen. The huge airplane spun three times in a circle before nose-diving into the ground.

Everyone cringed, then laughed. Even Chance.

"That kit cost me four hundred hard-earned dollars," Chance said, still laughing and enjoying the memories. "I bet I mowed ten dozen lawns to buy that plane and spent two months building it."

"And it only took him ten minutes to crash it." Ivan smiled fondly at Chance. "His mother went right out and used her green stamp collection to buy him another one."

Speaking of Mom, Chance hoped maybe she'd be in the video, but she rarely took him flying his planes. That was a special thing he always did with Dad. Still, with Mary here, he could only hope Ivan would catch a glimpse of his late wife and remember that no woman could replace her.

Not even one as pretty and apparently dazzling to his dad as Chloe's mom.

"Come on, Midnight." Chance took him outside then came back in, swiping moisture off his nose. "It's sprinkling."

Midnight shook water droplets off, then plopped down.

Mary laughed again as the plane crashed a second time. "What happened there, Chance? Did you run out of fuel?"

Chance laughed, warming to Mary a shade because that statement sounded so much like something his mother would say, and with the same cheeky grin too. "No, ma'am. I ran out of altitude."

Rounds of laughter filled the room. Rumbles rolled in the distance, cutting into the camaraderie and fun.

Midnight's ears perked up. He whined and eyed the windows, then Chloe, who petted him with her toes since he was sprawled at her feet. "It's okay, boy."

But a large clap of thunder later caused the dog to yelp, run frantic circles around the table and pace the room.

"What on earth is wrong with him?" Mary started to stand, but a streak of lightning outside the window halted everyone. Another streak crashed so close the entire yard lit. A thunderous *boom* resounded. The windows rattled.

Midnight yelped, scurried then jumped over the table. He landed square in Ivan's lap and sat there trembling.

Chance expected Ivan to toss the still-wet "mutt" onto the floor, but instead, he blinked a couple times then threw his head back and laughed out loud for the first time since losing his wife.

"Midnight, down!" Chloe tried to drag the seventy-pound Lab off Ivan's lap, but he pressed closer to the older man. Chance tried to help Chloe get the dog off since they couldn't even see Ivan's face.

But Midnight pressed his paws into the couch and would…not…budge. Ivan must have gotten another kick out of that because the more they tried to drag the dog down, the more the dog scrambled backwards and dug himself into Ivan's lap. And the more Ivan laughed.

Mary covered her mouth. Chuckles slipped out.

Chloe issued the dog a firm look. "I'm sorry, Mr. Garrison. He's terrified of storms."

Ivan swiped tears. His jaw jiggled from laughing. "Does he leap in your lap at claps of thunder too?"

"Yes. And he won't usually move until the rain stops and the rainbow shows up."

Ivan laughed more. "I'm surprised he doesn't squish you. You're no bigger'n a twig."

Chance snapped his finger. "Midnight, down. Now."

Midnight tucked his head and pretended not to see.

"He's fine, son. Leave him be." Ivan's arms came around the dog in a patting hug. "It's okay, boy. I won't let that old thunder 'n' lightnin' git ya." Midnight swung his head toward Chance and Chloe, then tucked his chin and tail.

Ivan bent close to the dog's lowered ears. "And I won't let Chloe and Chance git ya either. No sir-ee."

Midnight peered at Chance and Chloe like, "Ha! See?"

Ivan kept laughing until Midnight placed a paw on his chest and licked his chin.

Chloe tapped his nose with her finger. "Midnight, no licking."

Chance pressed a hand to his mouth and suppressed a smile. While Chloe scolded the dog, Ivan deftly issued Midnight a constant clandestine stream of reassuring scratches and pats with his affected hand.

Brock turned his laptop so the others could see the

radar for southern Illinois. "Looks like we might be stuck here awhile. Radar's full-on red above Refuge and won't pass for a couple hours."

True to the radar, the raucous storm and torrential flooding that followed stranded Mary, Chloe and Brock.

"I hear you make chess sets," Mary said to Ivan. "Do you play too?"

"Did. Haven't in years." He rubbed his hand, slightly atrophied from lack of use. "Don't reckon it'd hurt me to try though." He flicked his chin toward Chance. "Hey boy, go into my room and get the big set out. The one we used for kids who have trouble holding the pieces."

For the next two hours, Mary and Ivan played chess while Brock loaded pictures from their fishing excursion onto his computer, running on battery. Images of Refuge River came up.

"You remember that bridge today?" Brock asked Chloe.

"Yeah. The nice new one?"

"Yeah. Here's what it looked like right after the collapse a couple of years ago."

Chloe let out a delicate gasp as images scrolled across the monitor. "I remember hearing about this. It was plastered all over the Chicago news for months." She turned slowly to eye Chance. "Wow. Your team was the one who got those people safely off, wasn't it?"

Chance felt like a rooster ready to strut. "Yeah, that was probably us."

"Probably you? You are one of those valiant men who risked their lives on that bridge to save a busload of schoolchildren. Aren't you, Chance Garrison? I'm standing in the presence of a national hero."

"Actually, international if you want to be technical about it." Ivan moved his rook forward.

Brock flipped to the next picture and Reece appeared.

Chloe bent in. "That's the little girl who took Mr. Maple. Ben and Amelia's daughter, right? And Hutton, the one with mosaic Down Syndrome who manages the kitchen at the B&B, is her older brother?"

"Actually, Reece is Ben's stepdaughter. He adopted her after he and Amelia married. Hutton is Ben's brother. He stays with them several months out of the year. Reece was on the bridge when it collapsed," Brock said.

Mary gasped. "My goodness. That must have been horrible for Ben! For all of you really."

"It's par for the course. We deal with 'horrible' every mission." Chance watched the pictures of his team and their families click by. The desire for a family of his own hit with bomb-caliber vengeance. The feeling was so strong he knew he couldn't compromise his determination to marry and start a family soon, while he was still young.

He slid a glance to Chloe. By the look on her face, she was afraid of that very thing. "Amelia must have had to give up a lot having Reece so young."

Brock studied Chloe carefully, then Chance, then

Chloe. "Amelia had a rough go at it for a while. But she wouldn't trade her daughter for anything. No dream could mean more than a family."

Chance cast Brock a look of thanks. He might have crossed over to the dark side and joined the ranks of the cupid posse, but his loyalty still rested concretely with Chance and the unbreakable bond of friendship and brotherhood they held as pararescue teammates.

Chloe rubbed her arms as though cold. Yet the house temperature was muggy since the storm knocked the power out long enough to shut off the air-conditioner. The lights flickered, then came back on with the electricity.

The storm abated enough that Midnight slipped off Ivan's lap. Ivan patted his head then motioned Chance to his side. "Next time you're at the sporting goods store, pick this mutt up a fishing vest. And drag mine out of storage while you're at it."

Chance eyed the dog, then Ivan. Wonder and God-centered worship erupted inside. "Does this mean you'll come fishing with us soon?"

"It means I'm gonna catch twice as many bass as you and Brock put together. I got nine months' wortha fishin' to catch up on."

Chloe grinned triumphantly. Mary's eyes sparkled. Brock squeezed Ivan's shoulder. "It's on. I'll even let you man the depth finder."

The week since the storm had passed mostly uneventfully, but right now Chloe was late. "Argh! Story of my life." After meeting with Mandy at

Refuge Memorial Hospital, Chloe was now on her way to pick up her mother so Mary could accompany her to Refuge City Hall. Once in town, Chloe pulled into her mother's driveway.

Mary got in and checked the dashboard clock. "True to form. If you're less than thirty minutes late, you're early."

"Mandy's morning surgery ran late."

"Does she seem busy? Today's my day off, but I can run in for a few hours if she's swamped."

"No, the other part-time woman there didn't seem frazzled."

"They must be fine then. How'd it go?"

Relief trickled through Chloe. "Refuge's hospital administration granted permission to bring my therapy dog to visit appropriate patients who will benefit from Midnight's contagious cheer."

"That's fabulous, Chloe!"

"Yeah, and this week I get to take him to the class-room of Celia and Amber's special-needs students again. I'm not sure who got a bigger kick out of that last week, Midnight or the children. Midnight's also working wonders on Ivan."

"Yes. Seems he's making extraordinary progress."

Chloe cleared her throat. "Also, he seems to cheer up when you pay attention to him." Ivan had invited them to lunch during times Chance trained at the gym and DZ.

"Oh, stop. That's silly. The man just lost his wife."

"Over nine months ago. Statistics show that a huge percentage of widowers remarry within a year."

Mary gasped. "As a woman I must say that's depressing. I'd hate the thought of my husband replacing me so soon."

Chloe lifted her shoulders. "God said it best: 'It's not good for man to be alone.'"

"Then why are you so resistant to dating Chance?"

Chloe's shoulders dropped and her eyebrows drooped. "I can't believe I'm hearing this from the woman who told me every day from the time I was two to make sure I attain all my dreams before I marry."

Mary paled. "Mothers aren't always right. Especially young ones who wrongly speak to their children out of their own pain because they think they don't have anybody else to talk to. Those words never should have touched your ears, Chloe. You should reconsider."

Her mother's words seared Chloe's heart. She'd built her life on the foundation of her mother's early advice.

Had it misled her?

For once the thought of a relationship with Chance felt freeing rather than constricting. But Chance had acted strange yesterday. Why? "Chance hardly said anything last night. Maybe he's mad at me."

"Not every man uses the silent treatment to make their anger known. Don't automatically assume people are displeased with you if there's a millisecond of silence."

"No offense to Dad, being he's gone and all, but I know that's why I turned out to be such a chatterbox."

"I love your talkative nature. I'm just sorry about how you got that way." Mary patted her cheeks.

"Where will you be while I'm in my meeting?"

"I'll be right down the street drinking coffee at Square Beans."

Mary parked and wished her daughter success, then exited the car and headed for the coffee shop. Chloe took a deep breath and headed toward Refuge City Hall.

As Chloe stepped toward the building, butterflies beat their wings in her stomach. Much of her hope rested on the people waiting for her inside. If she did not get unanimous support, her dreams for a Refuge clinic could be dashed.

An hour later, Chloe slunk out of the building, glad Mary had come. Rarely did Chloe need to cry on her mom's shoulders. It had been years, maybe even since her daddy died.

But the way that meeting went just now, she hoped Mary had a full cup of coffee and two listening ears for Chloe.

After failing to win over the city council one more time, Chloe now knew that divine intervention may be the only thing to convince those two stubborn people that her unconventional program was legit.

One look at Chloe, and Mary ordered coffee to go. They walked circles around the town "square" until Chloe spilled every detail of the meeting and her frustration.

"Don't let disappointment get you down. With something this progressive, there will be setbacks.

But these are roadblocks you can conquer. You're an overcomer, Chloe."

"With God's help. I know."

"So, chin up. We better go. You need to check on Midnight, and I should get home so I can rest before work tomorrow. Mandy's office is horrendously busy on Fridays."

"Parents bringing children in before the weekend?"

"Absolutely. And I don't blame them. I don't know why kids always decide to get sick on Saturdays." Mary ruffled Chloe's hair the way she did when Chloe was little. "Where is Midnight, by the way?"

"At the B&B. Brock offered to watch him for me so he doesn't have to stay cooped up in my unit."

"That's nice, considering his animal allergies."

"He said he'd be fine. He doesn't react to most dogs."

They arrived at Mary's. Chloe hugged her goodbye. "You're the best, Mom," Chloe said, and she meant it. She was so grateful she had a mom who cared. Had a mom, period. She thought of Chance and experienced empathy's ache. Chloe hugged her mom again. A tad tighter and a little longer this time.

"'Night, Chloe. Sweet dreams. Love you."

"Love you too."

Sweet dreams.

Why did those two words evoke images of a certain shy, strapping modern-day Samaritan?

And the biggest question of all: Could it be possible that dating Chance wouldn't mean giving up her dreams?

But the way Chance acted last night, maybe he'd changed his mind about wanting to see her. Chloe wracked her brain to figure out why he'd been so silent. Was he displeased with her over something?

Mary's words drifted back into Chloe's mind: *Don't automatically assume that people are mad at you just because they're silent.*

Even though Chloe now knew the route home by heart, she turned on her GPS just to hear a human-like voice.

"Destination, Refuge B&B. Twelve-point-five miles."

Chloe navigated the roads that were becoming home to her. Even the gorgeous woodsy scenery didn't relieve her of the niggling question: Was Chance mad at her?

"You've made a wrong turn. Recalculating route. Go back two blocks and turn south on Haven Str—"

Chloe reprogrammed the GPS to take the scenic route rather than the fastest.

Maybe that's what she needed to do in the course of life too. Chloe eyed her silent phone. He hadn't called today. *Don't auto-assume.*

Just then, her phone rang. Finally!

Then she saw Brock's number, and disappointment dogged her. She forced it from her voice as she answered, "Hey, how's Midnight?"

"Great."

"Why are you whispering?"

"Chance is here. How far out are you? Not that I'm in a hurry. He's anxious to see you. He's hanging out, helping me keep your spoiled canine assistant entertained."

Chance came to see her? Her pulse fluttered like those butterflies in her stomach had earlier. "On my way. Ten miles maybe."

"Good. I'll detain him."

"Thanks, Brock." The clandestine call disconnected, which probably meant Chance had walked back into the room.

Thrill roller-coastered through her that Chance had come to see her. It was becoming harder to fight off the part of her that wished things could work between them. What if she gave herself over to it? Would Chance treat her dreams like Dad had Mom's?

Or was Chance different? Was he what he claimed? Maybe it was time to take a *Chance*.

"Recalculating route. Detour imminent."

Chapter Twelve

"Bet she took a different route," Brock said to Chance and tossed a Frisbee to Midnight. "You know there are mega-roadwork delays in Refuge these days."

Midnight retrieved the whirling disc and deposited it at Chance's feet. He picked it up. "That's because the mayor's looking to retire." Chance tossed the Frisbee across the B&B's grassy yard. "You know, he's giving Chloe a tough time." Midnight went after it, then set it at Brock's feet.

He flung it for the dog again and passed Chance on his way to the steps. "Whew, it's hot. Time for a water break."

Chance removed his gaze from his watch. "What time did she say she'd be back?"

Brock grinned and opened the cooler on the B&B's white vinyl wraparound porch. "Anxious to see her?"

Chance's ears warmed. "A little."

"She said around now." He handed Chance bottled water.

Chance swigged. "How late is she?"

Brock swallowed and laughed. "About thirty minutes." He knelt and scratched Midnight behind the ears. "But that's okay, huh, buddy? We're having fun romping in the yard."

The dog panted his delight. Really panted.

"He's hot too. I'll get him some water." Chance swiped sweat from his brow and walked toward the water hose. He looked around for a bowl and then cupped his palms.

"You're planning to let the dog lick water out of your hands?" Brock's face distorted.

Chance shrugged. "Why not?"

"Dude, dog slobber. That's pretty gross."

Brock had a point. Chance rose. "Fine, I'll go get one of your bowls then." He smirked.

Brock pulled a worse face. "I'd rather he use your hands." A rumble at the end of the road sounded. Gravel dust kicked up behind Chloe's car coming up Pena's Landing.

Brock hurdled the rail. "Never mind. I'll get a bowl. You greet your girlfriend." He whistled. "Midnight, come."

The dog jumped the rail as Brock had and followed in tail-wagging frenzy toward his unit.

Chance twisted the empty bottle into a bow tie and tossed it at Brock's head. "She's not my girlfriend."

Smirking, Brock caught the bottle. "Right."

"Not that I wouldn't want her to be, but she has problems committing. In fact, her problems have problems." He laughed ruefully.

Brock paused at his door and looked at Chance, then looked at Chloe as she pulled in. Brock turned back to Chance and leveled his buddy with a head-strong look that Chance only saw on Brock's face in hostile combat situations during tense pilot rescues. "There's not a problem alive so insurmountable that the two of you can't get over it to be together. Besides, you have the Big Man upstairs on your side."

Words eluded Chance as Brock's passionately spoken words marched through his mind. It was the first time Chance could ever remember Brock refer-ring to God. Joy welled up and then doubled when Chloe stepped out of her car…and rushed at him.

"Whoa!" He opened his arms in time to catch her on impact. "Wow, it's not my birthday. What's this hug all a—"

Before he could finish, Chloe effectively and af-fectionately cut him off with a firm kiss on his lips, a kiss that sent his pulse skyrocketing and disman-tled all thought processes.

He tightened his arms around her, then lowered her feet to earth. Chance grinned and peered down at her. "What's going on, Chloe?"

"I'll watch the dog," Brock said, grinning. Which meant he'd witnessed the missile hug and high-caliber kiss.

Brock called Midnight back inside and closed the door.

"Let's go for a walk." Chloe tugged him toward the woodsy hiking trails behind the B&B.

"Hold on." Chance went to the cooler and grabbed two bottles of water. "I want this walk to last as long as possible." He grinned. "Especially if it contains any more spontaneous mow-you-over hugs and sweet, mind-blowing kisses."

Chloe blushed but reached down and grabbed the entire twelve-bottle cooler.

He eyed it and his brows rose.

She shrugged one shoulder. "I have a lot to say."

Chance laughed out loud and took the cooler.

She slugged his arm. "More than usual, I mean. This could take a while."

"This way," Chance said after a solid half hour of hiking at such a fast clip that talking had been impossible. "I want you to see the waterfall."

Chloe nodded and tried to steady her breathing. Chance slowed for her benefit, but he was hardly winded, proving Chloe hadn't been kidding when she said she didn't exercise. He hated to push her to the point of exertion, but he was anxious to hear what she had to say. He slowed his pace considerably.

"Thanks. You're in amazing shape," she gasped out in a wheeze. "I need to start doing aerobics."

He chuckled.

"I didn't really realize just how outstanding an athlete you are."

"Try combat athlete. You learn to run fast with bullets zinging over your head."

"I'm sure." She paused and gasped as the entrancing waterfall came into view.

He grinned, enjoying watching her drink in the

beauty as rushing water wove like long locks of liquid hair down the face of a gorgeous rockscape. "I figured you'd like it."

She went for the first dry rock she found and dropped down on it. "You may have to carry me down. I'm serious."

"Sorry. Guess I was going a little fast, huh?"

"Uh, a little?" She guzzled half a water bottle. "You practically sprinted here up all those steep inclines."

"You did a good job of keeping up." He sat beside her. "So what's on your mind, Chloe?"

She pulled her legs onto the huge rock and hugged her knees. "I need to know if you were mad at me yesterday."

He laughed. "Mad at you? For what?" He shifted his torso to face her more.

"Never mind. You just answered my question." She recapped her water.

He lifted one foot to the rock. "What gave you the impression I might be mad at you?"

"My dad."

"Your dad?"

"Yes." She shoved her hands through her bangs. "I need to talk about him."

"Okay. Shoot." He rested an elbow on his knee.

"I mean, I need to talk about a lot of stuff. But to start with, I need to vent about my dad and how he was and why I am how I am, so I can be sure you still want to try to put up with me."

Chance blinked a few times while all that registered. Then he lowered his water and scooted close. "Put up with you?" He brushed a hand along her disheveled bangs, tucking them behind her ear. "Is that how you think I see this?"

Her face dipped. "That's how I would if I were you."

He lifted her chin. "Chloe, you have n-no idea how I feel about you. Do you?"

Her eyes widened as he set his water down and brought his other hand up to cup her face. He bent and placed the world's most tender kiss on her lips. One that whispered of all the emotion his words were hard-pressed to express.

At first she resisted, but soon her mouth became as pliable as Ivan's clay beneath his formerly nimble fingers. Chance reluctantly pulled away before things got too heated and cut off this important conversation and rested his forehead on hers.

"Chloe, somehow, somewhere, my heart forgot."

"Forgot what?" She brought her hands up to cover his, still cupping the sides of her face, still forehead to forehead. Then he tilted her face so they were eye to eye. "Somewhere along the way my heart forgot to remember that we're only supposed to be friends."

Chloe stood abruptly and paced. Her arms flailed like Celia's when she got on a roll. "This, this, this just wasn't in my plans."

Laughing, he tugged her back down on the rock beside him.

"I want to date you, Chloe. I want us to be a couple, more than just friends. I want us to see where God leads us."

Hopefully, He'd lead them to be together. Forever.

He looked at Chloe that moment and knew. No question. He wanted her to be the one.

The big question was whether she'd be the *best* one. Chloe didn't want children until she was older.

Chloe compressed her mouth and tried to figure the best way to explain her feelings to Chance. She never had a problem being direct but she didn't want to dishonor Dad, even in his death.

She caught Chance staring at her with the most tender, wonder-filled expression, so riveting it yanked her mind away from what she was about to say.

"Tell me about your dad, Chloe."

She hugged her knees. "He was a pastor who put his flock before his family. He could never see that we were severely lacking attention because of his outrageous devotion to his job."

Chance nodded at her to continue.

"That was his identity. He spent so much time with the church and so little time with his family that we all suffered."

"And he died never owning up to it?"

"Yes. What bothers me almost the most is that not one of those parishioners saw how neglected we were. They constantly called, constantly came by, needing this or that from him. Taking all of his time. When he died, so did the church."

"That's not right. But you know that. Is that why you have a hard time plugging into a church?"

"Absolutely. I trust God. It's people who are iffy."

She laughed, then grew serious. "I know it's not funny."

"If it makes you feel better, the church I go to, Refuge Community, is set up differently. It doesn't revolve around one man. It delegates tasks to group leaders and does everything in its power to preserve pastors' family lives and nourish their marriages."

She took that in a moment. "Mom desperately wanted a greenhouse. It could have brought in much-needed money because he gave financially back to the church to the point Mom couldn't buy me school clothes or supplies. Because of his compulsive devotion to his job and all he demanded of my mom for his flock's sake, she couldn't put the necessary time and money into the greenhouse. See why I am concerned about you and me?"

"Chloe, honestly, I don't see what this has to do with me."

"There will always be someone who needs you more than me. People trapped in disaster. Pilots in need of rescue. And you can't tell your team you're not going. Am I right?"

"Right. But we only have maybe five real out-of-country rescues per year. The rest are training ops."

"Or natural disasters, all of which are unforeseen." She stretched her legs.

"I won't be gone constantly."

"You don't know that. Besides, you have the heart of a pastor. I see evidence of it everywhere. I'm sorry but I can't live with that kind of loneliness, and I can't put my children through it. I don't want my kids to need a dad who is not able or willing to be there."

"Chloe, I'm more than willing and able. Only on rare occasions I won't be. And PJs retire early."

"That's the same thing my dad said. He was there all right, but always for others and never for us." She pulled her legs up again and clutched her knees to her chest.

"I want to reach out to youth. It's important to me, yes, but I would never let it come before my family."

"Right. That's what most ministers think going into it. Then before they know it, they're emotionally divorced from their wives and children. I even ran away once. Mostly to see if he loved me enough to come after me."

"Did he?"

"Surprisingly, yes. It was the one and only time he talked heart-to-heart with me. He promised that once he retired he'd spend more time with me and Mom. That promise was the only thing that kept her from divorcing him. But he never made it come true. He just dangled it in front of us until his death." Her jaw hardened.

"I'm sorry, Chloe."

"He'd preach about husbands loving their wives, then come home and ignore his family until he retired to the grave. The day he died my parents had gotten in the worst argument ever. Though it wasn't her fault, after Dad's death Mom spiraled into a depression. I talked her into using his life insurance money to buy her greenhouse. Doctors said that, plus having me and her joy over our animals, saved her from suicide."

"Did that give you the animal-assisted therapy idea?"

"Yes. But by that time Mom had lived through enough misery to convince me never to make her mistake of letting a man get in the way of my dreams."

"Chloe, I hate to break it to you, but Mary told me the second time we went fishing that she hopes we end up together."

"Figures. The traitor." Chloe gave a wry grin. "Speaking of fishing, is your dad going tomorrow, Chance?"

"Far as I know. Now stop changing the subject and tell me what you're so scared of."

"My biggest fear?"

As the words left Chloe's lips, she felt as if she were glimpsing it right in his gorgeous face. Because if there were ever a man she'd want to marry, Chance was the one.

"Following my mother's footsteps."

Chapter Thirteen

"Wait, Mom! I can't keep up." Chloe trailed Mary down the dock, unwrapping Midnight's leash which kept tangling in her wristwatch. Chloe kicked the branch aside that had nearly caused her to trip.

Unfortunately, the branch landed in the water rather than on the bank beside the dock.

The dog caught sight of the thrown branch. His body tensed, then rocketed off the dock to fetch it.

Chloe's body gave one big jerk. The leash loop caught on the industrial-sized watch her mother and Mal had gone in together to get her because of her tendency to be late. The floating dock tilted one way, then the other. Chloe overcorrected. Her arms flailed, but she couldn't loosen the leash. The dog splashed into the water after the stick, and Chloe splashed right behind him.

"Chloe!" Chance dashed for her, but it was too late.

A shock of water rushed over her head. Chloe

clamped her mouth shut, held her breath and desperately tried to untangle her watch from Midnight's leash. She wasn't fast enough. He dragged her farther underwater. Her blouse caught on deadwood and the leash tightened around her throbbing wrist. She jerked on the leash, on her blouse and fought panic. How long could she hold her breath?

Another splash sounded, nearby but muted.

Chloe clenched her mouth shut and flailed underwater only to come up and bump the underside of something big. Her eyes burned as she opened them in the murky water. All she could see was a large, wavy, distorted square. Must be the floating dock above her. No space between its hard foam underbelly and the water's top for air pockets.

Lungs screaming for oxygen, Chloe thrashed around, still submerged, looking for the fastest way out. Pulse racing she searched, frantically and futilely, for the closest side to sunlight. But she couldn't find a break in the water.

"Where is she?" Her mother's strained voice sounded distant in Chloe's ears.

Don't take a breath! Don't breathe or you'll die.

Her eyes felt ready to bulge out of her head. Cheeks strained, she continued to hold her breath, twisting her body, trying to dive back down and out from under the bobbing dock. Her hair snagged on something underneath the dock and held her there.

Okay, now it was time to panic. She opened her mouth instinctively to scream for help. Big mistake. Water rushed in.

She jerked at her hair and thrashed to keep from coughing or breathing while struggling frantically. She had to breathe, had to breathe, had to breathe right now. She bubbled water out. It didn't help. She was so dizzy now. She needed to inhale.

Something big disturbed the water beside her and disentangled her hair. Everything became surreal.

Strong arms enfolded her body. Warmth tugged her with massive strength to the right, opposite the direction she thought the surface was. The person holding her gave a mighty shove, and her face broke through water.

She sputtered and coughed. Brock reached down from the dock and pulled her up by the underarms. From the water, her rescuer Chance pushed her up with mighty oaklike arms. Then he pressed his hands on the wood planks beside her and pulled himself up in one motion onto the rocking dock.

Chloe rolled onto her back and fought the burning in her lungs. "Ugh." She pounded her chest. "'Urts!"

"Try to cough the water out, Chloe. Draw slow, light breaths so you don't pull the fluid deeper, then forcefully cough." Speaking of forceful, Chance's voice was just that.

She coughed and coughed some more, then couldn't stop.

Chance, kneeling over her, turned her face to the side. Then rolled her body sideways.

He must have known before she did what was coming next, because two milliseconds later she vomited frothy water.

"Oh, my goodness. She almost drowned!" Covered in convulsive tremors, Mary dropped to Chloe's side.

Chance handed Chloe a piece of cloth to wipe her mouth. She realized after using it that he'd shed his shirt. "She just swallowed a little water. She's fine."

Brock put a calming hand on Mary for which Chloe was glad. What seemed like an hour later but was really only a few minutes, Chloe slowly, with Chance's help, sat upright. Heat filled her face, as she croaked, "Please, no one tell me what an idiotic move that was." Her chest still burned from having held her breath for so long and gulping water at the end. "I'm the epitome of embarrassed right now. Stupid watch!"

Mary's hands flew to her mouth. "That did it?"

"Yes, Mom. You and Mal out to off me or what?" Chloe glared at Chance. "Do not tell me you told me so, buster. I did not wrap the leash around my wrist."

Now somewhere between bewildered and bemused, Mary blinked. Brock's mouth twitched. He covered it with his hand.

Chance bit back a grin and made zipping motions over his mouth. Concern still trumped humor in his handsome face.

Just then, Midnight trotted up to Chloe and dropped the stupid, offensive, death-trap branch in her lap.

Chloe made groaning sounds, then burst out laughing, mostly to keep from crying which made her cough again. "Okay, boy. Good job," she said when she caught her breath again. "I know you thought I was tossing it out there for you to retrieve. But next time we try that trick, let's not have my watch wrapped in your leash, okay?"

Chance stood and reached for Chloe's arms. He tugged her up and brushed her off. Brock handed her a towel from a hatch in his boat.

"Thanks. And I know you all want to laugh. So don't let me hold you back."

While Mary's mouth twitched, her eyes still held unshed tears. Chloe had scared the daylights out of her mom today.

"I'm just glad your dad wasn't here to witness this," Chloe said to Chance. "He might have had another stroke."

Chance chuckled but it still lacked humor, proving she'd shaken him. "Doubt it. He probably would've ripped stitches in his britches trying to help you. He's toughened up the past several weeks, thanks to you and Midnight."

"Then why won't he come fishing with us on Saturdays?" Chloe asked.

Chance's ears turned red. "I didn't ask him."

"I bet I can get him to come," Mary said with confidence that drew everyone's attention.

Chance angled his head. "Yeah, I'm sure you could."

Chloe looked from Brock to Chance to her mother, who blushed. "We've been going to bingo together."

Chloe craned her neck. "You and Ivan?"

"Yes. And we've been enjoying ourselves a lot."

"Like, a romantic kind of enjoying?" Brock paused.

Mary shrugged. "We'll see where it goes."

"Mom, why didn't you tell me?" Chloe hugged her, then laughed when Brock started teasing Mary.

But while everyone else chuckled or at least smiled, Chance walked away somber and silent.

Brock noticed right when Chloe did. His grin faded. "Hold up, guys. Something's wrong. Chance looks peeved."

Mary frowned. "Oh dear. I suppose Ivan didn't tell him we've been seeing each other during times Chance has training operations and meetings. Chloe, go talk to him."

Brock halted her. "No, clearly he's upset. Let me go."

"I feel terrible about this." Mary wrung her hands.

"Mom, are you happy?"

"Yes. Happier than I've been in a while."

"Is Ivan happy?"

"Seems to be. Says he is. He keeps asking me out." Mary shook her head. "But I can't compromise things between you and Chance."

"What's to compromise?"

"Don't lie to yourself, Chloe. And don't miss the chance of a lifetime. Literally."

"If this is what Ivan wants and Chance can't handle it, maybe we're not meant to be."

Mary shook her head. "I don't believe that for a minute. Nor should you."

"That would be fine except for the most important

thing—that he's intent on being a youth pastor and I'm intent on not being a pastor's wife."

Mary began to say something but clamped her mouth shut when Brock and Chance, whose conversation looked pretty intense, started back toward them. Brock broke off.

Chloe stepped away from Mary to approach Chance alone. "You okay?"

Chance studied her a moment, then shrugged. Though they stood mere inches apart, he felt a million miles away.

"Chance?"

Spears of annoyance streaked across his eyes.

"Please talk to me," she whispered, fighting the familiar sense of desperation that any silence provoked.

He eyed her mom and frowned slightly as his gaze returned to Chloe. "What do you want me to say?"

"The truth. How you feel."

His face transformed into something ruthless and determined. Chloe glimpsed the side of Chance that was the tough-as-titanium, search-and-rescue commando in combat. "How I feel? Like I can't believe this is happening so soon. How can he just replace her like that? Especially with the anniversary of her death looming. It hasn't even been one year." He shook his head and clenched his jaw.

"Chance, I'm sorry this hurts and makes you angry."

"I'll live with it if forced to. But don't expect me to like it—or the fact that you're so ready to write me off just because I want to help young people."

What could she say to that? Absolutely nothing, because he was exactly right.

Sadness coated Chloe like the mildew under the dock that had almost drowned her.

"It's just because it's coming up on a year, Chloe. Trust me. That's a hard day. He'll come around." Mary put on a full pot of coffee, which meant it'd be a long night.

Chloe refused to tell her mother that Chance hadn't called her since the fishing trip nearly a week ago. He hadn't even come by to see Brock, which cemented her deduction that he was avoiding her, probably so he didn't have to think of their parents together. Telling Mary would put a damper on her joy over her budding relationship with Ivan.

Chloe splayed all of her Chicago program's financial data on the table. Mary had agreed to come over and go through it and give fundraising ideas.

"I've wracked my brain over Refuge City Council's reticence for weeks. Well, two members' reluctance in particular."

Chloe felt a headache coming on. She popped two ibuprofin, then she set two coffee mugs on the counter and hauled out the richest tub of chocolate she owned. A day like today called for the good stuff and lots of it.

Mary turned around and saw the industrial-sized bucket of sweetness, then burst out laughing.

Chloe shook her head and listened to the gentle gurgle of her neon-green coffeepot and enjoyed the rich aroma. She plucked candy out of the tub and set out computer diagrams of the facilities she planned to have built.

"Your orthodontist is going to have a fit."

"He won't know unless you tell him." Chloe popped a chocolate into her mouth and extended the tub to Mary.

She shook her head. "No thank you. I'm trying to watch my weight. I want to lose a few pounds."

Chloe chewed slower. "Wow. You and Ivan must be serious."

"What makes you say that?"

"Drama mama, the chocolate fiend, is going without? You're serious about that guy."

Mary ignored her daughter's comment and reached for the papers Chloe spread out. "Is this all of it?"

"Yes. Everything." Chloe popped a seedless grape into her mouth to offset the chocolate. Or at least to make her feel less guilty later for the cocoa binge. "So, Mom. Back to Chance. You really think he'll come around?"

"About Ivan and me? I do." Mary's eyebrows pinched as she looked at the diagrams, then went through the spreadsheet and council minutes.

"Do you think he's right for me?"

Mary looked up and smiled briefly before running through the plans again. "I really do, Chloe. I think God's favor rests on both of you in this relationship."

Chloe eyed the chocolate, then the grapes, then went for the chocolate. She resisted the urge to chatter on about Chance. She didn't want to distract her mom from helping.

After all, Mary had built her own business and had heaped helpful advice that thrust Chloe up the ladder of the Chicago-based team. Now Chloe was in charge of building one from the foundation up. Problem was, she needed more people and money and clearance than she had now.

Mary stopped, stretched her fingers and resumed typing numbers in. She ate a grape but eyed the chocolate.

Chloe pushed the bowl in front of her mom. "It'd make me feel better if someone else indulged with me."

Snorting, Mary bypassed the chocolate and grabbed another grape. Her face twisted more with every punch of the keypad. Mary finally set the calculator aside and made a growling noise. "Let me see the accounting records. I'm afraid you don't have enough here."

"Records?"

Mary hesitated. "You must have cash flow to get things off the ground in case Refuge City Council denies the funding that your Chicago supers said you could count on." She peered over her glasses at Chloe. "Do you have any cash flow? Or were you counting on the council?"

"Was I counting on it? Yeah. Pretty much." Chloe suddenly felt ill. Possibly from eating so much chocolate, but probably because Mary was coming to the same depressing conclusion as Chloe and Mallory. Chloe reached for a grape.

Mary flipped through papers and became more agitated with each ledger. She opened the expense summary and frowned, then removed her glasses and let them dangle from the chain holding them. "Hand over that chocolate. We're going to be here a while. You guys need to have a backup plan for funding in case Refuge refuses to budge with grants."

Bone weariness clung to Chloe like a second skin. "Why must everything be so stinkin' hard?" Chloe started to put the chocolate away.

Mary tugged the bowl back. "You're not a wimp. And neither is Mallory. Chin up. You two'll get through this. The people and animals your program will help will be worth every pothole. The best road isn't always the easy one."

Chapter Fourteen

"Son, if you wanted the easy way, you shoulda joined the Girl Scouts, not the Air Force Special Operations Forces." Petrowski whistled into the new recruit's ear. "Hold it!"

The recruit puffed air out his mouth and tried to raise his face above muddy water while scrambling across the deep creek bed. Vince, who sat on his back while he crawled across slippery sections of creek, filed his fingernails, which teed off the new recruit even more.

"Dude!" He spewed trashy words and water. "You're too flipping heavy!"

"If you can't carry me across this creek, Airman, how are you going to swim a shot-up pilot from a shot-down plane across two kilometers of head-deep river? Move!"

Joel faced the recruits. "Who's next?"

No one moved. All of the camo-cloaked eyes bugged.

"Amazing. Days ago you flimsies were fighting to go."

"We didn't know how hard it'd be. Let us have a break," one recruit was brave enough—or foolish enough—to yell.

"Break on a mission and someone's guaranteed to die."

Chance tried not to grin. He'd gone through this. Every member of their elite team had gone through this. Despite feeling like death at times, they all made it through. The fifth day, with little sleep, little food and rationed water was always the toughest.

Some guys had already started hallucinating from heat, exhaustion, hunger, thirst and the physical exertion. But such was Special Ops training.

Petrowski walked, hands behind his back in drill sergeant fashion, in front of the line. "You gonna be in the more-than-ninety percent who wimp out? Or the top ten who dare make it? Your choice."

Joel followed Petrowski. "We believe in you or you wouldn't be here. You're a select few. Handpicked by us. Who's gonna step up their game and get through this?"

One kid who looked half brave, half scared, sloshed forward and lifted a timid hand. "I wanna make it. I wanna be a PJ. And I want it bad. I'll go next."

Joel pulled the first kid out of the water and patted him on the back. "You made it. Nice job."

The kid promptly bent over and cough-puked up whatever he'd swallowed, possibly a tree frog, when

Vince had shoved his face under the water every few feet. "With all due respect, sirs, this doesn't feel like training to me."

"No? What's it feel like, Airman?" Petrowski asked.

He cast a hateful look at Vince. "Like he was doing his best to drown me, sir."

"He was." Petrowski's chin rose. "But since it didn't work, get back in line. Unless you wanna go home to Mama."

"Sir, no, sir. I'm not wimping out."

Petrowski grinned. "That's my boy."

The kid released another barking hack. "By the way, sir, my mama's dead. But if she were here she'd kick my you-know-what for quitting on you like that."

"Good. At least one of your parents had sense enough to believe in you. Back in the creek you go."

Vince stepped into waist-deep water and intercepted. Pulled out his maroon beret and popped it on the young man's head. "Like how that feels?"

"Sir, yes. Very much, sir. More than anything."

"Then do what it takes to earn one. I know you can."

"Yes, sir." He swallowed, then peeled the beret off and respectfully returned it to Vince. "I'll surpass my best."

"That's more like it." Vince folded the beret and stuck it back in his chest pocket. "By the way, I would not have let you drown. We don't leave our teammates down there to die. You believe me,

Airman? Trust that I will do everything in my power to keep you alive?"

"Yes, sir."

"I need to know the same about you. Because when you're on the field, no one is going to be able to carry your weight for you."

Joel faced the group. "Reardon's right. All of you need to learn to lug the dead weight of a man who could be twice your size and combative from hypoxia related to hemorrhage-level blood loss, plus weapons and medical gear."

"Copy that, sir. I'll go again. Put Brock on my back this time."

Vince laughed out loud. "I like this kid." He faced Brock. "Hey, bro, I think he just called you a tank."

Brock smiled and flexed his muscles. Everyone knew he was the largest guy on the team, weightwise. A solid wall of muscle, not an ounce of fat anywhere, yet Brock always complained about his freckles and chipmunk cheeks. "Brutal honesty free of charge, compliments of Reardon."

Everyone laughed at that.

Chance hopped on the second young man's back, clicked the stopwatch and blew his whistle.

Though it was a bumpy ride, the kid made it in half the time. Of course, Chance didn't have the heart to shove his face in as much as Vince. Still, the recruit came up sputtering a few times. But this was as realistic as it could get as far as swim-crawling a victim to safety through a hostile, raging river.

The recruit's teammates clapped as he came out.

"Can I go again?" Even breathing hard, he had a determined light in his eyes Chance hadn't seen in a while.

Chance eyed Petrowski. He nodded. Chance waded back into the water and motioned to the kid. "Come on then."

Despite having already been through the strenuous exercise, the recruit shot like an RPG back into the water.

Chance hopped on his back and immediately started to shove his face under but paused to look up at Joel.

Joel moved close and nodded. "Go ahead. Push him, Garrison." Chance recognized that Joel also saw potential in this kid and wanted to see what he'd do under more insane pressure.

Chance pressed, then started to let off.

Petrowski shook his head. "Don't go easy on him."

Though Nolan was the most softhearted on their team as far as training the new recruits, Chance came a close second to Ben. The rest of the guys were hardballs. But the recruits needed that just as much as the occasional leeway.

"Step it up," Chance said when the recruit slowed for a breath. "You're being primed for the real deal."

The recruit grunted and sloshed on hands and knees. It was the PJs' job to test them under harsh pressure and see how they coped with intense physical and emotional stress. Because no enemy alive would have one mite of the mercy the PJ trainers did even in their most brutal moments.

"Toss me that." Chance nodded to a sandbag. Brock tossed it in Chance's lap, making him instantly heavier.

The kid, strained and winded, thrashed in place, then burst up and said something cocky, something about betting he could swim circles around Chance. Then he added something about how the sandbag could probably swim circles around Chance.

Chance shoved his face back under the water. And left it. Then Chance laughed. He liked this kid.

The recruit moved faster but didn't try to buck Chance off, which meant he'd incited Chance on purpose to ramp up the challenge. Chance grinned as they passed Petrowski. "This one just might make it." He still had his hand over the young man's head, and the recruit kept crawling for the finish. The pressure pushed him to excel. Good sign.

Petrowski walked with them. "Three minutes?"

"Over." Chance lifted his hand so the young man could have a breath. But the recruit kept his face underwater.

Joel laughed. "He's determined enough. Be sure to pull him up before he passes out."

Chance nodded and eyed his watch. Going on four minutes and the kid was still going strong. Strange sounds were coming out of him, like blubbering under water, but hey, whatever it took to get through.

Petrowski walked the bank monitoring them. "Make him team leader of these recruits. Build his morale. My gut says he's the type to step up his game with the responsibility. Maybe he can get these other guys to eat a can of Man-up."

Chance laughed because that sounded like something Chloe would say. At the end of the stream, Chance hopped off the kid's back and helped him from the water.

He rose, heaving air. "Wha-what was my time, sir?"

Chance eyed his stopwatch. "Under seven minutes to get down the stream. A record. You also held your breath the longest. Go see Petrowski. He wants a word with you."

The recruit's face blanched. "Is he kicking me off for insubordination?"

"Why's that?"

"I called you all sorts of bad names."

"I didn't hear it."

"That's because I spewed all of it underwater."

Chance laughed and clamped a hand on the recruit's shoulder. "You're all right. But now I know why you stayed under so long. Just don't tell Petrowski that."

"Am I in trouble? 'Cause I really wanna be a PJ."

"You're not in trouble. You're being promoted to team leader. Go see Petrowski. He'll give you instructions."

The young man's face lit. "Me? Really?"

"Really. Now go before we change our mind."

The kid, grinning wider than the river mouth feeding the stream, started to bolt toward their commander but spiraled back around. Slammed full frontal force impact into Chance and wound arms around his waist.

Took Chance a second to realize the kid was giving him some sort of clumsy, grateful, father-son-style hug and not a pathetically ineffective football tackle.

Which Chance knew took a ton of guts with all the other recruits and PJs watching. Uncustomary emotion surged in Chance, a longing to have sons of his own. He patted the young man's back. "I think you're gonna make it."

Respect glimmered in the recruit's eyes. "Coming from you, that speaks tons, man. Means a lot. Thanks, dude, uh, sir. No one's ever told me anything like that before."

Chance watched the kid go. A lump filled his throat.

The young man reminded him of former street thugs Val and Vince mentored in their neighborhood, ones that Rowan, the edgy youth pastor at his church, had inspired Chance to reach out to.

Sun beating on his back, Chance decided to make this kid his special mission. He'd do everything in his power to equip him for the PJ pipeline.

They'd been out here for five horrendously hot, humiliating, dreadful days. And not one young man had quit. That meant their PJ recruit vetting process at the DZ was working.

Chance thought of home. And of Chloe. And why those two always merged together in his mind. He hadn't had the opportunity to tell her he was leaving because Petrowski'd dragged their boots out of bed in the middle of the night and flown them here to the Smokies for a week of pop-quiz training. It kept the seasoned PJs on their toes too.

Chance needed to apologize to Mary and Chloe. He'd acted like a jerk about Dad. It was still hard. But being out here put things in perspective. At least Dad still had life left in his body. How he lived it was none of Chance's business. Not in the realm of romance anyway. If Mary made him happy, then Chance would learn to like it. No, love it.

If Chance was going to bully these PJ recruits into not shrinking back from the hard road, he needed to be willing to man-up too. He had no problem excelling in his military, paramedic and rescue career. But in civilian life? Another story altogether.

He'd go back and tell Chloe how he felt. He would let her know he was ready to accept whatever happened between Mary and Ivan. He would even try to be happy about it. After all, Mary had given his dad lots to live and rehab for, something to look forward to.

Chance watched the sappy street-thug PJ trainee. He was meant to reach out to these kinds of kids. Rowan had asked Vince and Chance to help lead the boys in the youth group, and he longed to do it. But the catch to be part of their church leadership was that they had to be ordained.

Chance knew it was something God was asking him to do. He could help young men in the military, like these and future recruits, and in civilian life the hoards of teens that frequented the DZ because they considered the PJs international heroes.

The way the youth group was growing, God's favor was there. Chance wanted to be a part of it, to make a difference, to encourage as many as he could. He wanted to convince them they could make it despite every negative thing they'd been told.

The recruit met each PJ's gaze. "No one's ever told me anything good about myself. Just that I'm not worth much. Thanks for taking time to train us and for serving."

Chance's heart went out to the kid. Totally.

Today had been the first time someone had shown this young guy he could be somebody and make something useful of his life. More than useful. Extraordinary.

This one kid alone was reason enough for Chance to take his suffocating grief by the throat and gut it out.

How many more men was he destined to help? A dozen stood right in front of him. Though the PJs pushed these guys past the grueling max, never once did they tell the recruits they wouldn't make it.

If they failed, it was their own doing. The team did everything within their power to prevent it. That was part of Joel's mantra and what made him such a good leader. He was all about imparting hope and not crushing spirits.

Especially not one, like this kid, who wasn't much younger than Chance, yet who'd already been disabled by derogatory words. Chance had a lot to be thankful for.

He couldn't imagine growing up with a dad who didn't fully believe in him. Or one who never said a kind word or encouraged him in whatever he tried.

For that reason alone, he'd be happy for Dad. Mary wasn't Mom, but she was a fine woman and she'd raised a fine daughter. *Very* fine.

Chance cleared his throat. No more taking the easy road. He was going home and making Chloe his, no matter what unseen hand tried to shove his face below murky water.

He wasn't giving up on her. No more easy way.

"You're thinking about Chloe." Brock smirked.

"What makes you say that?"

"You look all pathetic and dazed, like you're wandering around your own little Wonderland looking for Alice."

"You're just jealous." Chance snorted. "Chance, does she have a friend? Does she have a friend? Can she find a friend for me? You ask me like fifty times a day."

Brock headlocked him. "Watch it! I'll swing my ban hammer over your head. I don't need a woman to make me happy. Not one woman, anyway."

Chance wrestled free. "Did Petrowski hold your head underwater too long yesterday or what?" Chance knuckled Brock's buzzed red head. "Because that might be the only unpathetic excuse you'd have for not realizing what's so wrong with what you just said."

Brock play-shoved him. "Hey, back off. You just stay in Wonderland, and I'll have my own private tea parties, minus the tea, with twice as many waitresses now that you're off the dating scene."

The others grinned at their good-natured razzing.

Chance straightened. "Who says I'm off the scene?"

"That receipt for a seriously expensive ring that I found in your Jeep and the fact that I'm ticked off you didn't tell me about it."

Chance dipped his head, but Brock wasn't done.

"Also the fact that you and Chloe have been exclusive for a while. Unless you're holding out on me about that too." Brock feigned hurt. "PJs don't keep secrets from each other. Especially not us."

"Man, I'm sorry. I just wasn't sure. I bought the ring on a whim and thought about taking it back several times."

"Chicken. *Bwok-bok-bok.* You know you want this."

"But does she?"

"You'll never know until you ask. As Petrowski put it, drink a can of Man-up. Ask her."

"She might say no."

"She might. But so what? Since when have you ever taken the easy way, Garrison?"

True. "Fine. I'll ask her."

"Congrats, bro. Hope she says yes."

"Me too." Though Chloe still claimed misgivings, Chance was praying that God had been working on her.

"Don't flake, or I'll never let you forget. You'll live in PJ infamy with *Bwok-bok-bok* as your call sign."

Chance laughed. "I won't chicken out."

Now, if Chance could just locate that illustrious, elusive can of Man-up.

No more easy way.

Chapter Fifteen

"We never thought it would be the easy way," Mallory said on the phone to Chloe the next weekend.

"I know you're right." The easy way was avoidance—Chloe's tendency where romantic commitment was concerned. The hard way would be to call Chance up right now and blurt out how she felt.

"What's the worst thing that could happen?"

"I don't know. I could make a fool of myself, I guess."

Mallory snickered. "Since when has that bothered you?"

"Fine. Stop griping at me so I can get off the phone with you and do it while I've got the guts."

Mallory let out a shriek and Chloe couldn't help smiling. "Don't celebrate yet. He may not want to be with me. I haven't seen or heard from him in a week. I haven't seen Brock, either, so Chance hasn't been by here. Maybe they are on a training mission or he's doing something else with the PJs, but still… you'd think he could find a phone. He was calling twice a day for months."

"There has to be a good reason. Something came up."

"Yeah, like his intelligence."

Mallory giggled. "Can you ask Ivan where he is?"

"I guess so. It's just, Ivan didn't offer the info and I like to keep our visits professional rather than personal."

"In other words, Ivan might figure out you like his son, something that is obvious to everyone already, Chloe."

Chloe laughed. "Chance probably finally figured out he should run as fast and as far from me as possible."

"I doubt that. Don't think the worst."

"Sorry. I am conditioned to expect the worst. That's what Mom and I got from Dad. After so many years of him rejecting my pleas for attention, it hurts too much to hope for more."

"God has something good for you, Chloe. Hope."

"All right. I'll hope, and you pray!"

"You know it. I'm also praying about the Refuge clinic situation. Mindy put in her notice here, but I'll just try to cover for her. Bert won't like it, but too bad. He's unreasonable. Have you heard from the vet yet?"

"Yeah, that's a no-go. And I am still waiting to hear a verdict on a business license too. I'll call you as soon as I do."

"Sounds good. Love you. Call me as soon as you talk to Chance. I mean it. Even if it's three in the morning. I want to know."

"Will do. Have you considered what I said about Bert yet? His reluctance to set a date and the fact that he keeps trying to wrench every dream you've worked for away?"

A sigh. "Clow-eee. Enough. But since you took my advice, I'll pray about it. Seriously. I will ask God to show me the truth if I'm not seeing it."

"Good. Love you too. Tell your mom to call her sister. Mom has good news to share. Freaky news."

"About Ivan? She already told Linda. How do you and Chance feel about all that?"

"I'm okay with it. Happy for them. Ivan now works much harder at therapy. Mom's given him a reason to shape up and rehabilitate. So even if nothing comes of it, they're both in each other's life for good reason."

"And Chance?"

"God's working on him. But he's having a hard time. Partly because the anniversary of his mom's death is looming. Tomorrow, in fact."

"Could be why you haven't heard from him. Reach out to him, Chloe. He'll appreciate that."

"Thanks, Mal. 'Bye."

After hanging up, Chloe called Chance. It was the first time she'd initiated a call. He'd always called her before. Shimmers of shame sprinkled her that she hadn't appreciated his effort.

His voice mail picked up. She scrambled for what message to leave.

"Hi, Chance. This is Chloe. I've been missing you and wondered if you'd be interested in going fishing with us tomorrow. I know it'll be a tough day, so it might help if you don't spend it alone. My mom and your dad will be there, so I understand if you don't wanna come. But, I hope to see you."

I love you.

Chloe swallowed against the words trying to spring from her heart and out of her mouth.

Tears sprang to her eyes as she clutched the phone to keep from saying it. Why couldn't she just tell him how she felt? Was she afraid he found her too annoying after all, too much of a chatterbox? Did she fear he'd changed his mind?

"We're meeting at two at the usual place. You know, in case you decide to go. Well, it seems I'm rambling. Good to hear your voice, even if only by answering machine. I've missed it. Missed you. 'Bye."

Chloe slammed her phone shut and groaned. Midnight stood to attention. Chloe dropped her head to the table and bumped her forehead against the wood.

She raised her face and groaned again.

Midnight's head cocked sideways.

"I know, boy. And yes, you're right. I'm going crazy. Crazy in love and crazy without him. And after that bumbling, rambling, desperate-sounding message, there's no way he'll show. No way on earth."

Images flashed through Chloe's mind of her

showing off her best tricks in front of her dad and him growing annoyed. If her own dad, a pastor and supposed master at doling out grace, couldn't put up with her boisterous, attention-starved nature, there was no way a quietly observant, highly disciplined military icon like Chance could.

"What did he see in me anyway?"

Clearly, she'd just made a complete fool of herself on the phone. He'd be a fool to show. If he did, it would likely be only because he felt sorry for her.

"He'll be a no-show, buddy. I know he will. And I don't blame him. But I had to at least try, ya know?"

Chloe drew a breath and hauled out her paperwork. She'd worked on it late into the night and still couldn't reconcile how to get past Steele and Bunyan.

It seemed since stepping foot inside Refuge she'd slammed into a series of brick walls every which way she turned.

God's way isn't the easy way. The thought came unbidden, but there it was.

"Midnight, do you suppose that's true? Am I exactly where I need to be? Or have I seriously missed the boat?"

She flipped on the radio to listen for weekend weather forecasts. A local Christian radio announcer's voice wafted through her living room, stopping her cold and warming her heart. The message riveted her to the spot.

"Congratulations if you're enduring hardship. Deciphering God's will through circumstance is one of the most difficult ways to hear God's voice. But getting to know Him, and His voice, will be worth it in the end."

The program ended and Chloe readied Midnight for a bath. A dreaded task considering he fought her every step of the way. For a moment she considered bopping down the boardwalk and asking Brock for help with the big dog, who would undoubtedly wrestle his way out of her tub before he was clean and free of soap.

She went to the window and didn't see his sports car, which could mean he'd gone to work out with Chance.

Chance. Her heart melted and stung at the same time.

Then she remembered that she hadn't seen Brock's car all week. Not that she was trying to catch glimpses of Chance or anything. Ha!

She returned to the bathroom. Midnight was nowhere to be found, customary when tub-filling time came.

"I know all your hiding places by now, buddy. Don't fight me on this. You're stinky and this bath is overdue."

She checked the water. Adjusted the temperature and thought about the radio message that seemed directly targeted at her.

"Thank You for being so gracious to remind me. I don't know how I so easily forget that everything in life points to the chief end of knowing You better. And the more I get to know You, the more I wish I'd known You sooner. I want to be in a place where I really, really know You, Lord. Even if I have to go through hard things to get there, You're worth it."

Tears dripped into the water and she grabbed a tissue. Thumping sounded in the living room. Either Midnight forgot he was supposed to be hiding, or he needed to go out and was whomping his whale of a tail on the door.

She stepped out of the bathroom and tumbled over a huge, black unmovable blob surrounded by hundreds of puffy, floating white things.

"Argh!" She caught herself as the wall flew toward her. "Midnight! Why did you shred my favorite feather pillow? Ugh." She knew bath retaliation when she saw it.

"What are you sitting here in the hall for?" He licked her knees as she rose. "Furthermore, if you're here instead of hiding, who's at the door? And why didn't you bark?"

She headed to answer it. Midnight followed, panting.

"Could be an intruder and you'd lick them to death."

Chloe opened the door.

And gasped.

The most fearsome-looking, but cutest Rambo she'd ever seen stood on the other side.

Chance had never seen a more welcome sight. After Chloe had left him that message a bit ago, he had to come see her. He hadn't even taken time to change out of his camo.

Even his face was still covered in war paint from playing air gun games at the DZ, the PJs' treat to the recruits for making it through a week of grueling training.

He smiled because he'd heard her griping at the dog on the way to the door. He'd never tire of Chloe's extroverted nature or extreme talkativeness.

Her face filled with shock and awe.

"Hi, Chloe." He grinned.

Her eyes widened. "Oh, hi. Come on in." She stepped aside. "Wow, you look, uh, rather scary."

"I just got home. I've been on a training op all week." He stepped in.

She averted her gaze. "Oh, Ivan didn't mention it."

"Probably didn't want you to worry."

"I'm getting ready to give Midnight a bath. You could help me if you want. He's really a booger when it comes to bubbles."

The dog eyed Chance carefully, then cowered behind Chloe. Chance laughed.

"See? I'd be the one fending off an intruder. He's one big chicken."

At that word, Chance's face changed. He studied her intently, then knelt to pet Midnight. "I know the feeling."

"So, wow. You really are a top-notch soldier."

He grinned. "Airman."

"Airman? Okay, so Air Force dudes are Airmen. You really have guns and everything?"

"Not on me, but yes. I have weapons."

"Wow. I'd like to see them sometime. Unless of course it's illegal or something, with your top secret status."

He grinned. "Special Operations."

"Got it. Well, I'll eventually learn the terminology, you know, because what you do is important to me, well, because you're important to me, and I want to know more about your life, and—I'm rambling again, aren't I?"

Chance stepped closer. She was talking even more rapid-fire than usual. He gauged her body language.

Nervous.

He smiled and stepped closer.

She took an involuntary step backward.

"So here you are, coming to my rescue again. You have perfect timing because he's a brute when it comes to being bathed, and I normally am the one to get drenched, and he never really gets clean because he's so big and I'm so—"

"Beautiful." Chance pulled her close and kissed a period onto the end of her anxiety-induced marathon run-on sentence.

After another lingering kiss, she broke off and peered into his eyes. "I didn't know when I'd see you again."

"I was on an unplanned training op. I couldn't call for various reasons, one being my personal cell drowned in a river mishap and died. It's now in the shop."

"Okay." She pressed her lips together as though to keep from chattering.

He grew quiet too. They stared at one another silently for an endless moment, then Chance cleared his throat. "When I get nervous, I tend to clam up."

"That's okay," she whispered. "When I get nervous, I'll talk enough for both of us."

"Which means we'd make a great team."

Her eyes blinked rapidly, scared to believe.

"I got your message from earlier."

"How?" Her lips compressed together as though determined to listen more than talk.

"I programmed calls to forward to my military phone. And for the record, I've missed you too."

"Will you come fishing with us tomorrow?"

He tried not to stiffen. "I don't know."

"Thanks for being honest."

"Always." He stepped back and looked down her hallway. Midnight lapped up water from the hall tiles. Chance's body tensed and he bolted past her. "Heads up. Bathwater's running over." He sped there and shut off the faucet.

"Oh, man! It's all your fault." She laughed. "You look amazing in uniform, and all that camouflage and face paint distracted me from my tub-filling, dog-washing mission."

He grinned and tugged on Midnight. "Come on, boy. Let's get this over with."

Midnight got the most pathetic look on his face and whined as Chance and Chloe slid his stubborn seat across the wet tile and into the bathroom. All four legs skittered in a last-ditch effort to flee.

They laughed and slipped and slid as Midnight tried to scramble up and run away from them and especially the tub.

"Why's he so scared of it?"

"I'm not sure."

"Think someone abused him with hot water or something?"

Chloe's face looked stricken. "I'm not sure. How did you know he was abused?"

"You rescue at-risk animals. I saw the scars on his neck one day you came to Dad's. Two plus two…"

"Maybe we shouldn't bathe him then. I hate to bring back bad memories if someone did try to burn him with water or drown him." She looked terribly distraught.

Downplay, downplay. He never should have opened his trap. "Many dogs are simply frightened of water."

"But he's a water retriever and he certainly had no problem going in the other day to bring back the branch that almost caused me to drown," she said with a laugh.

Chance laughed too. That's one of the many things he loved about her, that she could laugh at herself and that she didn't take herself or anything else too seriously. "True. Maybe it's just the tub. But he'll eventually learn that we're not going to harm him and that baths can be pleasant."

"We?"

His cheeks warmed. "Yeah. I plan to help you with him as much as possible."

"I'm being too chatty. Aren't I?"

"No." He laughed and bent to plant a tender kiss on her cheek. "The water's getting cold."

But not his feet.

"I have an idea." Chance tossed three of Midnight's rubber balls in the tub.

Midnight shot forward to retrieve but stopped at the edge of the tub and made throaty noises. He slashed desperately disgruntled eyes at Chance and barked at the water before panting playfully.

"I don't think he's traumatized by the tub. I think he simply doesn't like taking a bath." He believed it too.

"C'mon, boy. Time to get it over with." They pulled Midnight over the edge. He splashed violently. Chance wrapped arms around his neck and spoke soothing words in his ear. Midnight calmed to nervous wriggles and finally sat.

So still that Chloe laughed. "Look at his ears. He's not happy right now. He looks either humiliated or mad."

Chance chuckled. "He'll get over it. Long as you give him treats afterward."

At the word "treats" Midnight's ears and countenance perked up.

"Soon, buddy. Ya gotta get clean first."

They began the process of bathing him. True to Chloe's prediction, the dog split as soon as they got him good and sudsy. Chance grabbed at him as he leaped through his and Chloe's arms. His body knocked Chloe back as he bolted for the bathroom door. Chance shielded her.

Midnight's soppy tail slapped Chance's face and poked his eye on the way out. Chance laughed. "Touché, buddy. I deserved that for not rescuing you from the dreaded bath."

They rushed after him. Chance got to him first,

touch-tackling him in the hall and laughing as Midnight shimmied and shook sudsy water all over everything, including them.

Then he went calmly, willingly, back into the tub.

"Chloe, honest, I think he's playing. I think he just likes to fling suds all over your walls and knick-knacks and stuff." Chance poured cups of clean water on Midnight until all the bubbles were erased.

"Did you know Celia Pena has a cat she calls Psych?"

Chance laughed. "I did know that. She spoils him but tries to make everyone think she's not into cats."

"Did you know Mina's the cupid posse ringleader and Celia is second-in-command?"

Her baiting him reloaded his confidence ammo. He grinned.

"What's so funny?"

He shook his head. "Nothing. Tell me about Midnight's early life."

"Why do I get the feeling you're avoiding the romance conversation?" Chloe gave Midnight his after-bath treat.

Chance scrubbed her scalp, tousling her hair in the process. "You're too smart for your own good." His fingers tingled from the silky strands. He removed his hand and sat on her couch, then smiled because her hair was still mussed when she stepped into the kitchen to pour tea.

"Yum," he said when she handed him a cup of horrid-smelling stuff, but he was referring to the way her tousled tresses rested in wild waves around her beautiful cheeks, bright eyes and burgundy lips.

Chance concentrated his gaze there, then forced himself to look away. "I missed you, Chloe." Missed kissing her crazy too. In addition, his deep feelings for her had multiplied exponentially in his absence.

He longed to hold her and not let go.

She might have perceived the direction of his thoughts because her cheeks tinged and she sat farther on the couch from him than usual. Probably good considering the docile Midnight was their only chaperone.

She started chattering, which was just fine with him since his mind had missile-locked in on the way her lips changed shape when she talked rather than on what she was actually saying. He forced himself to listen to her words rather than revel in the mechanics of her mouth.

Wrapped in his paw-print bath towel, Midnight chomped a rawhide bone and nestled contentedly on Chance's feet.

"Your dad did phenomenal work during his therapy this week."

"That's what he said when I got back."

"He mentioned you're moving the last of his stuff to Refuge in the morning."

"Yeah. It's just coincidence but kind of symbolic that it lined up on the one-year anniversary. But that's the only day the new owner could meet me at the house. She's a single mom. The house'll be a good home for her and her kids. Dad gave her a killer deal on it. He had tons of equity built up."

"So financially he's okay?"

"Yeah. I think he's getting more used to Refuge and starting to think of it as home. Your mom has a lot to do with that."

Chloe nodded. "Does it bother you too terribly that they're going fishing tomorrow, of all days?" Her face jerked as though her own words offended her. She smacked a hand on her forehead. "I'm sorry, that was the world's dumbest question."

"No, it wasn't. You're just being sensitive because you know I'm having a tough time with the idea. I'm glad he has something other than grief to look forward to tomorrow."

"I'm sure it'll still be a hard day for both of you."

"Yeah, but at least he'll have your mom there to ease it."

"And you too, you know."

"Whether I can go will depend on when I get back from bringing the rest of his stuff from St. Louis. Ben offered to drive me and use Manny's truck to haul stuff. Ben lost his dad a few years back. I think he offered because he sympathizes with me."

His entire team had offered to help. But with Chance being one to more easily process things quietly, the fewer people around him when he packed away the last of Mom's stuff, the better.

"If you decide to go fishing with us, let me know and we'll wait to leave until you get back. I have to meet with the city council again before we can hit the water anyway."

Chance nodded and hated that his mind marched

miles away. He could tell it would mean a lot to Chloe if he'd go. He just needed to get through tomorrow.

Then he could focus on her and him and their programs.

He eyed her finger and thought about the ring he'd purchased in haste but hopefully not in waste. He was sure she was the one he wanted. He'd wait as long as he could. Hopefully, she'd come around. If not, he'd return the ring and donate the money anonymously to her program.

Celia had gotten the ring size for him by getting Chloe to try on her ring.

Chance scratched his cheek and came away with a blackish-green smear on his fingers. Reminded him he was still covered in face paint and fermented combat fatigues.

Chloe didn't seem to mind. He did, though. If he was starting to be able to smell himself, it had to be bad.

"I'd better get home and shower and rest up. It will be a long day tomorrow." Long, hard day. He rose reluctantly. Being with her felt like being home. "I should go."

A sweet layer of thoughtfulness glazed Chloe's vivid eyes as she stepped forward and rested her hand on his forearm. "I could go with you tomorrow."

Chance studied her a moment, drinking in her kindness, stilled by her gentle touch. How something so simple could chase the army of dread advancing heavily he didn't know.

But he had an inkling he'd be at least a mild mess tomorrow, which meant she'd see him weak, and would leave him too vulnerable. Then he saw her swallow hard, causing him to realize that by offering to be there for him she'd advanced into unchartered emotional territory herself.

He'd be a fool to resist or evade it.

His mouth locked up. He stepped close and curled his arm around her, hoping to communicate the gratitude he felt inside.

When words came back to him, he gave her one more squeeze. "Thanks, Chloe. I'd like that."

For a moment she looked at a loss for what to say, which was so untypical of her that he laughed. It felt good.

Her answering smile sat somewhere between sassy and sweet as she slipped, also reluctantly, in his opinion, away. "I'm glad."

Something magnetic tugged him toward her. He must have leaned that way because her eyes grew wide enough to stop him. "I should go." Really. Right now. Before he apprehended her in a commando hug that he hoped would hold her heart hostage for life. He swallowed at the enormity of his own thoughts. "Bye, Chloe." Though everything in him protested, he walked away.

She followed him to the door. "I'll see you tomorrow."

Tomorrow.

He stepped into the cool air. A moist breeze brushed his buzz as he jogged down the steps. Now at his car, he turned and peered over his shoulder at her, knowing she was out of hearing range but wanting to say something nonetheless.

"'Night, sweetness," he whispered softly.

Despite any logical reasons against it, he felt tethered to her like clips on a tandem harness.

Safe.

He felt it with her and knew she felt it with him.

If this is what starting to fall in love with someone felt like, he was staring into the face of free fall.

Should he pull the rip cord?

Or scramble back and succumb to safety?

Chance fastened his seat belt while questions raced.

His call.

It was not one he could make right now. Not with what he was facing tomorrow.

Chapter Sixteen

"I know what it feels like to lose one."

Chance swallowed what felt like a knotted piece of rescue rope settling in his throat at the kind words of his teammate and friend, Ben Dillinger. Earthy aftershave scents strengthened as Ben moved to stand beside him in the small living room Chance had grown up in.

He knew that by "losing one," Ben meant the childhood home as well as a parent since his family's home had burned down when Ben was a youngster.

Ben's words made Chance want to escape the profound sense of loss that had been dogging him all day and take a long walk in the woods. He'd visit the squirrels and deer around Refuge. Watching wildlife always relieved stress.

"Me too." Chloe moved closer to him. Her gaze brushed his mother's face in a framed picture with tenderness.

"Yeah, that's precisely the reason I want a family

soon. It's hard losing so many family members at this age, while I'm still young. I want my children to avoid that." Chance studied Chloe for a reaction, but all he could see was compassion as she studied his late mother's image.

"I'm sure she was as lovely a person inside as this picture shows outside."

Chance just nodded.

He carefully set the photo back in the box but couldn't bear yet to close the flap. "I always thought I was a s-s-strong p-person, until this—" Irritation drew Chance's eyebrows inward. What on earth was up with his incessant stuttering today?

Stress tightened the band of pressure that had wrapped around his chest last night as soon as he started dreading today.

"I thought I was doin' all right. Thought I'd licked this. Then I jolted awake in the middle of the night with some kind of weird p-panic attack. It's like I woke up and realized what a shock to my system everything's been and I hit rock bottom." Remnants of dizziness, nausea and tremors dogged him right now, in fact. "I've never felt so physically ill nor such gloom, doom and despair."

"Dude, you shoulda called me," Ben said.

Chance shrugged. "You have a family."

"You're also family, bro."

Chance laughed. "I doubt you would have brought me what I felt like I needed last night anyway. I couldn't pray. All I wanted was beer. And lots of it."

Chloe giggled. "That's normal. Did you drink?"

"No. I haven't kept alcohol in the house since I gave my life over to the Lord. But had it been there, I would have downed a case because I felt for several moments like I was seriously losing my mind."

Ben rested a hand on the pine bookshelf. "You went a week without sleep or proper nourishment for the training op. I'm sure that exacerbated it. Might be good you've hit rock bottom. Only way now is up."

"W-when will I st-top m-m-missing her?" Pushing the unbending words out of his mouth felt like shooting square bullets through a little round hole.

Chloe squeezed his hand. "Never. But it will get easier. No one can truly understand the pain of losing a parent until the weight of it sits on their shoulders."

Ben nodded. "She's right. And, dude, you've been burying this. It had to come out sooner or later."

Chance released a frustrated sigh. Today's sudden reappearance of the severe stuttering that had sent him into a shell of shyness as a boy didn't make things easier. He didn't need one more thing going wrong. Didn't God know that? Of course He did.

"Mom always t-told me that what doesn't kill me will make me st-t-ta-tr…" Chance gritted his teeth and tried to think of another suitable word. An easier one. Since when did he take the easy way? Since it had been too long for him to remember tricks his elementary school speech therapists had taught him that had cured him completely.

Or so he'd thought.

How could he train to be a back-up communications specialist with his PJ unit in the event teammate Vince couldn't be on a mission, and have a stutter?

Easy answer.

He couldn't. Period. Not possible.

Unless he beat it back into submission.

He'd conquer this thing once and for all. He would.

His parents always told him he could do anything he and God set his mind to. It had been a struggle for them to pay for his therapy when insurance didn't cover it back then. But Mom had known how important it was to him to overcome it. What would she think now that it had resurfaced? Probably she'd tell him what she said about any difficulty he faced. To quit sulking, get his big boy britches back on and beat it.

Chance's eyes veered back to the photo and left him wishing it was she in lively warm flesh instead of a flat and lifeless image that paled in comparison. "Is it weird for me to want to keep the answering machine?"

Chloe eyed it. "With her voice on it? Not at all."

"I still keep the last message my dad left on my voice mail. I listen to it from time to time," Ben agreed.

"Don't ever erase the message." Chloe brushed bangs from her eyes.

"Or ditch the machine," Ben said. "In fact, record her voice on DVD."

"It's the only way you'll hear her voice this side of Heaven." Chloe bent to retrieve another packing box.

"You go to church anywhere yet, Chloe?" Ben asked.

She froze. "No."

"Would you want to?"

"No." Her tone snapped enough to seem like they'd asked her if she'd ever robbed a bank or wanted to.

Ben caught Chance's gaze, then slipped from the room, probably to give them a chance to talk.

"Sorry." Chloe sighed. "Ben was just being nice. I overreacted."

"I understand."

"I don't know why. Not today. Let's not talk about me. Tell me what's going on with you. What are you thinking?"

He shrugged.

"It'll help to talk about it. Come on. Purge." She not only settled on the rug but tugged him down with her.

One look and he knew she really wanted to know.

He sat opposite her. "I wish I'd listened more when she was alive. Drank it in, you know. But everything happened so fast. I didn't want to believe she was dying. In retrospect I wish I'd been sponging up everything about her while she was still here."

"There's hope in all this. Don't forget. You'll see her again. Jesus is the ultimate answering machine. He made a way possible for you to hear her voice again."

Chance blinked at her.

"Dime for your thoughts."

"Wh-what happened to a p-penny?"

She smiled. "Inflation."

"I'm c-concerned about Brock. His p-parents will die someday. So will he. I want him to b-b-be there too, ya know? Any m-mission, one or all of us might not m-make it home."

"I know. So we just keep workin' on him and praying."

"H-h-have b-b-been p-p-p..." He huffed. "T-talking to God ab-b-bout Broccoli. A l-l-lot." The entire team had adopted Chance's nickname for Brock.

"How's your dad holding up today?" Chloe asked, probably to draw attention away from Chance's frustration over the sudden return of dysfluent speech.

Chance shrugged. "'Bout as well as c-can be expected."

Ben returned. "He still supposed to go fishing with Mary and Chloe today?" he asked when Chloe went to deep clean the bathroom for the new homeowners.

"They asked me along. Not sure I can be around the two of them today."

"Mary and Ivan?"

"Yeah. That re-reminds me. H-he never ret-t-turned my call. Sorry, B-Ben. Don't know why I'm s-stuttering again."

"Man, no sweat."

Chance redialed his father's phone number. No answer.

Two terrible claws of dread punched through

Chance's rib cage and clenched his lungs, then caved his chest, leaving little room for air. He hit Redial on his father's cell number. No answer there either.

Chance stared at the phone, willing Ivan. *Hear it.* If he wasn't answering either phone or returning calls, something could be very, very wrong. "Bro, I can't get him to answer. I never shoulda left him alone this morning. But he insisted he was fine."

Acutely perceptive, as was every member of their team, Ben must have picked up on his fear because he beckoned Chloe from the bathroom, plucked his keys from a sofa table and motioned Chance toward the door. "Let's go check on him."

Halfway to Refuge, Chance's phone rang. An enormous blast of relief hit when he saw his dad's caller ID.

"It's him." Chance answered the call. Maybe his dad had just decided to venture outside and didn't hear the phone or something. Which was an answer to—

"Hello? Chance? Oh, thank God!" The shrill panic in Mary's voice caused Chance to stiffen.

"Mary, what's wrong?"

Ben accelerated and listened carefully at the same time. Chloe grasped Chance's hand tightly and bit her lip.

"Chance, don't panic but the ambulance just came and picked up your dad."

The strangulating cord that was tightened around Chance's chest moved a suffocating tendril up to wrap around his throat.

Ben eyed Chance with caution and sped up to rates that would make even their friend Officer Stallings pull them over.

Chance tried to make his stubborn mule of a mouth and airless lungs work. "W-wh-what happened?"

"I don't know. He stood abruptly from the garden bench and flat passed out."

Chance was too frozen with fear to ask the inevitable.

Please. I can't go through it again. Not this soon.

"He came to about the time the EMTs arrived. Cole, the paramedic, gave me your military cell number and said I should call you but to tell you he thinks Ivan will be okay."

Chance took the deepest breath of his given life. "Good. That's good. Where'd they take him?"

"Refuge. I'm following in the car. I'll call you when I know something more."

"Okay." Chance hung up, feeling numb.

What if his dad had had another stroke? Would he recover?

Ben's hand on his shoulder made him look up but the maelstrom of possibilities, fear and panic wouldn't release his mind. Chloe, eyes closed, murmured soft prayers.

Questions flooded Ben's concerned eyes. PJs stuck together with a brotherly bond of unbreakable armor no weapon formed against them could pierce.

In fact, Chance had fractured his ankle on a bad landing during a team jump the year Manny crashed into the only grove of trees for miles at NASCAR speeds. Chance, still attached to his parachute, hadn't fully landed feet to earth before he'd started sprinting to Manny. He was the first one to him. Seeing him all busted up had done a real number on the team.

But it had also bonded them and made them realize how precious life was and how dangerous their jobs were, even between missions on hostile soil. Thankfully, Manny recovered, but he never forgot the way Chance refused to leave his side, even for his own painful ankle fracture. And Manny had been the first one by Chance's side when his mother passed on.

Chance knew without a doubt their team's Kevlar-thick bond had grown partly from the prayers of authentic Christian leaders, Joel Montgomery and Aaron Petrowski. Two of the strongest men, inside and out, that Chance had ever met, men who weren't ashamed to live their lives by faith.

The past few years, the seven-man team, eight with CO Petrowski, started falling into faith like dominoes.

Chance had been the most recent addition. Brock was the only holdout and while everyone had thought Vince would be the toughest cookie to convert, Chance knew Brock had a stubborn streak the length of the Mississippi.

Chance succumbed to the safety of silence. He concentrated a few composure-restoring moments on trees, power poles, electric lines scrolling by the Illinois interstate that would bring them back to Refuge. Chance leaned back on the headrest and closed his eyes. He sought God with his whole heart and being.

Chance knew Ben and Chloe understood the need. The moment. The silence. The grief trying to gobble him whole.

"Mary's n-not sure what h-happened. Cole Trevino, Refuge's paramedic, told her to tell me he thinks Dad will b-be okay. But what if he's h-h-had another stroke?" Chance squeezed his eyes against an unexpected and frustratingly strong torrent of tears that refused to be bottled up any longer. "Guys, I can't lose an-n-nother—"

His words were choked off by the fear and emotion that got the better of him. He never lost it like this. Never. He hadn't even cried at his mother's funeral. Well, maybe a tear. Or two. But no more. He couldn't. He had to be strong for his dad, who wasn't holding up well at all.

And now, Chance had to be even stronger, a tough feat when he felt like a paper-thin vase made of intricate porcelain that life had just flung violently from a fifteen-story window. There was no way he could land safely and survive this blow of losing his mom and now news of Dad's collapse.

Ben set the cruise control at just over the speed limit. No sense in risking their lives or others' to get to Chance's dad.

Chloe still held Chance's hand. Her silence surprised him.

"I could use a good dose of chatter about now," Chance said.

"God, please intervene," Ben said.

Chance fought the insane urge to laugh and

decided not to tell Ben he meant Chloe. But of course, Ben would pray. It's what he did, how he dealt. And right now, Chance needed a good helping of that too. Probably most of all.

Ben continued, "Right now, right here, in this car, in that ambulance, in that hospital, please intervene." Ben's normally calm voice carried an urgent air of authority as he began to release words that took Chance aback. He wasn't used to people praying out loud. Chloe nodded her head and held Chance's hand just a little bit tighter.

Chance agreed by closing his eyes and nodding as he listened to the rest of the words.

"You are the Giver of life and the Lifter of our heads. Step in right now and show Yourself strong. Be with Chance and Ivan." Ben broke into a spontaneous worship song.

Chloe looked up, then back down.

"Heal him, Lord, unless you have a better plan. We lift him up, Lord, to your wondrous hands. Lead us, Lord, to come alongside your work, and help us trust through things we cannot understand."

"Amen." Chance let the word flow from his mouth, along with a couple of renegade tears that wrestled for release. He opened his watery eyes to find Chloe watching.

She smiled so sweetly, it almost looked like she actually loved him.

Regardless, God did. He'd draw strength from that.

Chance envisioned himself as a little boy crawling

up in God's lap, just as he had with Ivan when he was little.

An enormous sense of peace washed over Chance and infused him with calm that didn't make sense in the midst of the call he had just received. How it happened, Chance wasn't sure. But every semblance of fear lifted.

If only this moment-by-moment missing of Mom would ease too.

A long-forgotten memory of his main speech therapist praying for him entered his mind. How had he forgotten about that? Had prayer made the difference?

If it worked back then, maybe it would work again now if the stutter didn't go back into remission after his stress level eased.

Six months ago Chance didn't have the assurance that he was firmly God's. But he had promised his mother when she'd become ill that he'd try to learn the ways of God, and Chance hadn't broken that promise. In retrospect, he wondered if she made him promise because she sensed she was going to die, even though doctors were convinced she'd recover.

The doctors had been wrong, but his mother had been exactly right about his need for God.

In seeking God, he had discovered that God had been chasing him for years. At least now Chance knew he had God's strength to rely on. Whatever he was about to face, whatever happened, he would get through it.

He had to.

His team depended on him, as did the people they risked their lives to rescue. People whose survival depended on every single member of their team being in top form, physically fit and of sound mind, will and emotions.

As if sensing the steel return to Chance's resolve despite facing the unknown, Ben squeezed Chance's shoulder and removed his hand. "God will help you, bud. No matter what hardship you have to walk through in this life, He won't let you walk it alone."

"And neither will we," Chloe whispered.

Chance swallowed at the sappy sentimentality. "Thanks." He'd never been more grateful for friendship. Chloe, Ben, the team and the abiding hope that had latched on to Chance's heart the day he'd handed it to Jesus made the difference. He just had to be reminded sometimes, and Ben's prayer had done that.

Ben reached for the radio knob. But before he turned the music back up, he got that goofy, poetic look that he always did before saying something profound. Chance knew deep down that what Ben was about to say was straight from the heart of God.

Ben said, "You're disoriented in an unforgiving blizzard so deep you can't see a way out."

That's exactly how he felt. How did Ben know?

Ben continued, "But spring will never cease to chase away the winter. Good things are bound to begin coming back into your life soon, Chance. Be ready for them to bloom."

* * *

"How is he?" Chance asked after arriving at Refuge Memorial Hospital.

Dr. Riviera issued a wry look over his glasses. "Other than spitting mad and hollering over missing his first fishing trip in a year? Fine as long as he doesn't stand up too fast again and bottom his blood pressure out."

"You're sure this wasn't another ministroke?" Chance asked. Chloe pulled her bottom lip in and moved closer to Chance, shoulder to shoulder. The silent comfort seeped calm into him. Made him wish he could pull her into his arms and soak in by osmosis her caring essence and sweet strength.

Riviera chuckled. "I'm one hundred percent sure. Just a harmless episode of orthostatic hypotension. We lowered the dosage on his blood pressure med."

Chloe eyed her watch.

Chance wound his arm around her shoulder and squeezed. "I know you have a meeting with Refuge City Council soon. Feel free to go on in and see Dad first."

Tenderness filled him as Chloe leaned into his arm like a bird taking shelter under its mother's wing. "Sure that's okay?" Chloe asked Dr. Riviera.

"Yes. In fact, he should be fine to finish out his day terrorizing the lake trout as long as someone's there."

Chance laughed, glad Riviera knew Dad well already. Stress fell off his shoulders like fifty-pound ammo packs. Especially when Chloe's arm came around his waist and squeezed back, reciprocating his hug.

"I'll see you later," she said and turned to go.

"Hope so." Chance watched her walk away until she stepped into Ivan's room. Amazing the peace her presence and God's calm cordoned within him. Like a three-strand rescue rope. Even now, he felt her prayer and His presence.

"What a scare." Mary tugged her purse strap over her shoulder. "I'm sorry to have frightened you, Chance."

"Understandable. It obviously scared you too."

That meant Chloe's mom really cared about Dad, which meant Chance needed to get his act together and come to a total acceptance of their relationship.

Chance leaned over and hugged her. "I'm glad you were there, and I hope this won't scare you off."

Tears filled her eyes, surprising him, but confirming how much she cared about Ivan and what Chance thought of them spending time together. She smiled and hugged him back. "Thank you, Chance."

Her hug felt motherly and for once that made him smile instead of scowl.

Chloe came out of the room chuckling, so no telling what Ivan said to her while she was in there. She waved to them on her way to the exit.

"Shall we?" Mary eyed Ivan's room.

"Ladies first." Chance motioned her gently on.

"I respect how hard this—situation—between me and your dad is for you," Mary said after they visited with Ivan for a long hour before stepping out to let him rest.

Chance grinned. "*Situation?* I'll bet you beat

Chloe and me to the altar." Chance only said it because Chloe was gone, engaged in battle with a couple of sauerkraut members of Refuge City Hall determined to doom her animal-assisted therapy program before it ever began.

As Chance's words registered, Mary gasped. "Are you thinking of proposing?"

"Not thinking about it." He pulled the jeweler's box out of his pocket and opened the lid. "I'm asking for your blessing."

Mary gaped at the ring. "It's beautiful!"

"So is your daughter. May I have her hand?"

Tears sprang to Mary's eyes. "I can't think of a worthier man to entrust her to, Chance. Unequivocally, yes."

Mary ogled the ring again.

"Oh, and about you and my dad. It's not as hard for me as it was a few weeks ago. You have my blessing too."

A few tight hugs later, Mary handed back the ring. "So when is this going to happen?"

"The proposal? I hope soon, but that depends on her. It's a secret. And I want it to be private, between Chloe and me. Sorry."

"I understand. I'm sure I'll hear all about it in vivid detail after it happens." Mary chuckled.

"You know your daughter well."

"Her dad never paid much attention to her."

"You didn't get much either, from what I hear."

"Yes, well, I coped with it better than she did. She was only a little bitty thing living to get one sliver of her daddy's attention. I'm glad you've made her feel worthwhile again."

"She means everything to me, Mary. I love her. And I guarantee she'll never be able to rid herself of my attention." He grinned.

"You're perfect." She patted his cheek.

"Not perfect. But I know how to love those I care for and I know how to care for those I love."

"Well, you're perfect for *her*. So I hope things progress soon. Will you be fishing with us today?"

No more easy way.

Chance studied Mary and could see it would mean a lot to her too. Plus, he didn't want to be far from Dad in case he had another episode before they got his blood pressure medicine regulated.

"Actually, I think I will. But don't tell Chloe I'm coming. I'll just show up and surprise her."

"I do like the way you think. See you at two. The sun won't be so fierce then and Ivan will have had a chance to rest up with a nap, so I won't feel too guilty about out-fishing him in his infirmity." She laughed.

Chance joined her. "I don't know. Even at his worst, he's pretty handy with a fishing pole."

She chuckled. "I don't doubt that. I'll drive him home from the hospital, if you don't mind."

"I don't mind. I need to go to the B&B and get my fishing gear from Brock's anyway."

"Which reminds me, where will you and Chloe live once you're married?"

"One thing at a time." Chance smiled. But in truth, he'd been pondering the same question. He knew for sure he wanted a big yard and lots of bedrooms for all the babies that would come along, hopefully soon.

An uneasy feeling curdled through him like sour milk.

He recalled Chloe saying she didn't want kids young, but he was counting on the fact that she loved him enough to compromise and meet in the middle with the timing of starting a family.

He was willing to put it off a little longer than he wanted. But the important question was if Chloe would be willing to step it up for him. Would she alter her preconceived calendar for the sake of a solid future with Chance?

Everything at this point depended on one thing: how Chance fared in her heart compared to the importance she put on her dreams.

His fingers curled around the ring in his pocket.

Chloe's tightly held plans and her adamant words about not wanting a family while she was young curled doubts around his mind.

His ring on her finger. Her dreams and plans.

Which meant more to her?

Or could they find a way for them to have it all?

Chapter Seventeen

"You came!" Chloe rushed Chance. He caught her and swung her around on impact.

What was it with Chloe and Mary and their linebacker hugs?

Chance set her down and bent over the fishing bucket nearby, staring at the wiggling worms inside. "You dig those up yourself?"

Her chin zoomed up. "I most certainly did. But I'll share them with you."

He lifted two foam containers. "I stopped at the bait shop on the way here."

"I bet my worms are bigger, which means I'll catch better fish."

"We'll see."

"Oh, baby…*it's on.*"

He loved the look of challenge in her eyes.

He reached for her left hand and ran a thumb along her ring finger. Her steps stuttered, and she tilted her face up. He kept his face forward and neutral and fought off the grin trying to tear his face in two.

Muah-ha-ha-ha-ha.

He couldn't wait until he could hold her hands and feel his promise banding her finger. Maybe by Christmas, if everything went as he planned. His mouth dried.

He was doing it. Really, really doing it.

Brock had teased him about backing down, which made Chance all the more determined to go through with what he knew he wanted for the rest of his life.

"Chloe, your mom and I laughed all the way here," Ivan said once they were all tucked securely in Brock's luxurious bass boat.

"Why's that?"

"Mary got to talking about your infamous fall in the water on that previous fishing trip. She told me about it. I'm glad you're okay after falling in."

"You mean when Midnight jerked me in when he went to retrieve the branch?" She laughed.

Everyone joined her. Chance was glad she could laugh about it now because it sure hadn't been funny then.

Chance watched his dad, who watched Chloe and Mary and smiled. Chance was glad his dad could find joy on what would have been an otherwise dreary day. Chloe changed the subject to Ivan's chess sets. Everyone laughed as she spouted funny ideas for chess piece themes.

Thank You for Chloe, Lord.

"You're explosively fun, Chloe." Chance decided right then that everyone needed a Chloe in their life.

He intentionally kept his shades on so he could drink her in without her awareness because he liked to watch her in unguarded states. She was actually subdued now. Why? It wasn't like Chloe to be quiet at all.

She looked so pretty silhouetted against the crystal-blue backdrop of Refuge Lake and the rustic surrounding woods. Her body swayed in a mesmerizing fashion as the boat bobbed gently on placid water under a clear, tranquil sky.

"Dude! You got a whale!" Brock yelled from across the boat.

Chance scrambled to his pole which nearly bent in half. "Whoa, there." He reeled and tugged and reeled and tugged and laughed at himself for becoming so immersed in Chloe that he hadn't noticed he'd hooked probably the biggest fish in the lake.

"You want the net?" Brock set his pole down and brought it over. "Looks like you're gonna need it." Brock drooled, watching Chance haul the monster fish in.

No matter how big the thing on the end of that hook, Chloe was the best catch of the day.

"Might be a humongous turtle," Ivan said then laughed.

"Seems so." Chance continued to work the fish. "Gimme the net."

At that moment Chance's line snapped and his weights flew back to smack him in the forehead.

Chloe laughed. "'Take that,' says the one that got away."

Chance rubbed the rapidly rising knot on his forehead and grinned crookedly, then eyed her pointedly. "The next one I hook, I don't plan to let get away."

She blinked a few times, then flashed a smile that could light the sky for a thousand inky nights.

Chance contentedly studied Refuge's beautiful horizon. Stately trees pointed like limb-feathered arrows to a sky painted today in cloudless pink and pastel-purples that streaked like a sunburst across a brilliant blue two shades lighter than the lake.

Brock eyed the sky too. "Perfect day for skydiving."

"Definitely," Chance agreed, knowing the only thing Brock enjoyed more than fishing was parachuting.

Ivan chuckled. "They both have free-fall DNA in their blood. I think these boys are twins separated at birth."

"Chloe, ever tried it?" Chance asked. He'd like to ask Chloe to go with him sometime on a tandem jump and experience the thrill of free-falling from his favorite place to be: the sky.

"No, but it sounds exciting. I've always wanted to try it, but I've never gotten the nerve up."

Brock ducked while Chance recast his reconstructed fishing line. "You should go sometime. Chance could hook you up, literally. You could tandem with him."

Chloe's eyes lit. "I'd like to. Mallory would freak. She's always wanted me to go with her."

Brock's ears perked up. "Mallory skydives?"

"Well, she never has but she's always wanted to. But she wants to go with someone she trusts. Her fiancé says to fly through the air without a plane around you is foolhardy. He puts a damper on everything in her life."

"Chloe!" Mary made tsking noises.

"Well, he does. I'm just stating a fact. He's becoming the kind of possessive men often get before they become abusers."

"Maybe I can take her tandem diving sometime with you and Chance," Brock offered.

"I have an even better idea. Why don't you take her fiancé skydiving, then forget to tell him how to pull the thingamabob that releases the parachute?"

Brock snorted.

Mary shook her head. "That girl. What am I to do with her?"

Ivan chuckled. "Nothing you can do but keep loving that mean streak out of her." Ivan winked at Chloe. "Although I happen to think she's all right just the way she is. Nothing wrong with looking out for someone you love who may be headed in the wrong direction."

For whatever reason, Chloe's eyes filled with tears.

Everyone froze. Ivan looked at Mary for help. She shrugged and eyed Chloe, then Chance and nodded her head.

Scooting closer, he slipped an arm around her waist. "Something bothering you?"

"Partly yes and no. It just felt strange Ivan saying

that. I mean that in a good way. It was almost like I had a dad who actually cared there for a second."

Chance swallowed and nodded. "Dad does care."

Chloe seemed composed now so Chance shifted slightly, reading her body cues to see if he needed to remove his arm. But she leaned into him instead of away.

Joy flitted through him like the minnows in Ivan's bucket. "So it wouldn't be such a bad thing to have my grumpy old man for a stepdad?" *Or father-in-law.*

She laughed. "I can't believe that just came out of your mouth, but no. He's a delight and he gives sage advice. I've never had that from a fatherly perspective. Amazing how it's improved my outlook."

"So what was it that bothered you?"

"I'm concerned about Mal. She sounded despondent when she called today. Her fiancé threatened to take back the ring if she didn't give up her volunteer spot on the rescue team. Rescue's all she's ever wanted to do. If she can't cover Mindy, I have to move back to Chicago immediately."

Mary raised her head and listened carefully.

"Mal is devastated because he gave her an ultimatum."

"No pun intended but that sounds fishy," Ivan said.

Brock listened intently, taking it all in, but didn't comment. He'd been in a controlling relationship before so Chance knew he could identify with Mal's situation.

Chloe sighed. "And, worse, she suspects he's cheating because she won't sleep with him. She's thinking of hiring an investigator to prove or disprove it."

"I know a good one. Petrowski's sister Ash is a PI-turned-skip tracer," Brock said.

Chance nodded. "Yeah. Ash would love in on this. I'll give you her contact info when we get back."

"Thanks. Anyway, just pray for her. This is all so dreary. Let's change the subject, shall we?" Chloe stretched out to relax, but Chance knew her well enough now to know tension dimmed the wattage in her smile. He cast her an understanding expression. She winked. His heart flipped like a banked fish.

"So, Mary. Give us some dirt on Chloe." Brock smirked.

"Mom doesn't have any dirt." Chloe smirked back. "I was a perfect child. Still am."

For whatever reason, Midnight lifted his head, stared at her, then gave a loud bark.

"See? Even he knows you." Chance petted the dog.

Mary snorted.

"Hush, whistle-dog, or I'll turn you into a pair of cat slippers." Chloe scrubbed Midnight's ears when she said it.

Mary faced Chance. "Has she told you about the time she got mad at her dad and turned to trouble when she was sixteen? I mean real trouble."

"What, like you mean with boys?" Chance teased.

Chloe choked out a laugh. "No. Police."

Chance settled back. "I have to hear this."

"Me and Mal were always saving animals. We had

a massive collection of butterfly nets. We'd run around the neighborhood with Mallory's red wagon saving moths and bugs from drowning in people's pools. Well, except for spiders and bees. I squashed those when Mal wasn't looking. But she drew the line at flies and mosquitoes."

Chance laughed. Brock grinned.

"We'd rescue anything in trouble. We found a set of kittens someone dumped off in a box at the city trash pit once. We rescued them, then bathed them."

"With my best body wash, I might add. Then they hid them in her father's study," Mary finished.

"He found them and took them to the animal shelter and told me they'd be humanely discarded." Chloe scowled. Chance could see snatches of the strong-willed, softhearted little girl she must have been back then.

Mary clicked her tongue. "She cried all day. I felt so sorry for her."

"But not sorry enough to defy Dad and go rescue the kittens. So me and Mal sneaked out in the middle of the night and set some animals loose from the local pound."

"Correction. They set *all* the animals loose."

"Well, it wasn't a no-kill shelter!" Chloe laughed.

Mary shook her head and eyed Chance like, "See what you're getting yourself into and who you're dealing with?"

"The first time we did it, I got a warning. The second time we didn't get caught. The third time we got booked."

Chance leaned forward. "Third time?"

"Yeah, I guess I'm a slow learner sometimes."

"Sometimes?" Mary exclaimed, laughing. "You're the valedictorian of the School of Hard Knocks."

Chloe laughed. "Then Mal's my salutatorian. We're co-conspirators. She's the animal rescuer I got my Lab from."

"You have more than Midnight?"

"I have Midnight. Mal has a potbellied pig named Penelope. We'll add more animals when we get my program off the ground."

"A potbellied pig? That's kinda cool. Any relation to the guinea pig?" Brock helped Ivan untangle Mary's line from a thick green patch of yellow-flowered lily pads.

"Nope. Completely different species."

Brock nodded. "Mallory sounds interesting."

"She's definitely that. She's got the spunky girl thing going on."

"Wow. Brock's into that," Chance whispered. "And he goes gaga over redheads." He scratched his jaw and eyed Brock.

"I know what you're thinking, Chance, but we can't do it. We can't try to set them up when Mallory is engaged to another man, even if he is the biggest jerk in the world. We just have to pray that God shows her before she makes the biggest mistake of her life."

"Speaking of relationships, I need you to under-stand something about me. I have plans too, plans that I can't put off for very long. If I do, my dad will never know his grandchildren. I don't want to grow old or even die before having grandchildren. And I don't want my future children to miss out knowing their parents and their grandparents."

"You're still young, Chance."

"Yes, I am in my mid-twenties, like you, but it's already too late for my children to know my mom. The longer I wait, the better the chance that more relatives will be gone, since all my aunts and uncles are my parents' age."

"I understand. I also understand that sometimes life throws us on a different route than we expected. And sometimes, God is the one navigating that change. I think if this is meant to be, we both need to recalculate what we had preplanned and be open to a divine detour."

"So we'll stay surrendered to His will and roll with the changes? You'll be willing to follow the path God puts us on, Chloe, whether that's together or not? I like that. At least we'll know we're running hard after Him."

Her lips trembled and she looked like she could laugh and cry at the same time. He chuckled and pulled her close for a safe, quick hug. "I know this is a scary step for you, Chloe. I know it. But one thing I've learned about God is that He's trustworthy. His love is steadfast no matter what you go through."

"And you've been through a lot the last six months."

"Yeah. The initial stages of grieving were extremely tough. I'd come to cope okay until I figured out Dad had a thing for your mom. I'm not going to lie to you and tell you that wasn't hard."

Chloe's heart thudded. "You wouldn't be happy for them?"

"I'm not saying that." They docked the boat. Brock helped Mary and Ivan out. Chloe and Chance watched as they walked to a park bench and Mary sat close to Ivan. He leaned on her.

"Your mom has also been through losing a spouse, which I know helps Dad. I'm just saying that seeing him interested in someone besides my mother was one of the hardest things to witness. And well, since their feelings for each other have obviously been growing, it's felt flat-out weird. Yet not in a bad way, I know. Just weird, especially if you and I, you know, find our relationship to be, well, permanent."

"That would be odd to have you as both my boyfriend and my stepbrother." She grimaced, mostly at the thought that maybe God had brought Chance into her life so Ivan could meet Mary. That would be fine except for the deep feelings she now felt for Chance. Maybe God didn't have Chance in mind for Chloe. Depressing thought.

"Or worse, I could be your husband and your stepbrother. And your father-in-law would be your stepdad." His voice had adopted a testing, teasing tone.

"I told you, Ivan wouldn't make a half-bad dad."

"So, what about me?" he asked tentatively. "Would I make a half-bad husband?"

She smiled, then tried to hide it.

He grinned. "What? You got an ornery look just then."

Her face warmed. "That would depend on your definition of *bad*."

His brows rose. "Why, Chloe Callett, I do believe you're flirting with me." Something in his eyes changed, and he brushed a thumb along her left ring finger again.

Why did he keep doing that? Was it on purpose? Not knowing was driving Chloe nuts.

Chloe stepped back, and Chance advanced then chased her around a tree. She giggled and squealed. Once he caught her, the smoldering, slightly dangerous look in his eyes receded and a look of deep and gentle caring replaced it.

"You'll never be able to outrun me, so get used to getting caught." One of his eyebrows arched.

"Maybe. Maybe not. I decided to take the plunge, bite the bullet."

His other eyebrow rose to meet the first. "What bullet is that?"

"I bought a treadmill."

He doubled over laughing.

"I'm going to start exercising three hours a day."

His laugh died. "Three hours?"

"Okay, two."

"Every single day?"

"What? You don't think I can?"

"I just don't want you to have too-high expectations of yourself and then fail."

"Are you calling me a couch potato?"

"Depends. Do you own a couch?"

She clobbered his shoulder. "Correction. Are you calling me a chair tomato?"

"No."

"Good, because—"

"I'm saying if you overdo it on the treadmill, you're likely to hurt yourself."

"But aerobic exercise is good for the heart."

"Fine, start slow and gradually build to your goal."

"I'll do two hours, five days a week. Does that sound reasonable?"

"I think you should start out with twenty minutes a day, three times a week and go from there."

"Fine. But then I'm not walking the whole time. I'm going to run. I'm determined to get up that waterfall at least half as fast as you do without getting winded."

"Sounds reasonable. Have you ever run on a treadmill before?"

"Well, not exactly. But how hard can it be?"

Chance stayed silent.

"Speaking of waterfall, let's hike there," Chloe said.

They bid goodbye to their parents and drove to the B&B. "Where is it?" Chance asked as they headed up the leafy stone-riddled hill.

"What?"

"Your treadmill."

"Still at the store. They're delivering it late today. You and Brock can help me unload it.

Anyway, back to your dad and my mom. You're sure you'll be okay if, you know, things progress between our parents?"

He pulled her close but not close enough to be considered putting the moves on her. "Seriously, as hard as it would be to see Mom replaced, I'd be okay with it as long as I knew it was something sifted through God's filtering hands. I can handle anything in life as long as I know that He sanctioned or allowed it for some good reason or higher cause."

She nodded and enjoyed the feel of his high morals and physical strength protecting her—even from themselves. She appreciated the fact that he didn't try to ravish her like that flash in his eyes said he wanted to when she'd foolishly teased him. Where were a bucket of ashes and a wad of sackcloth when she needed it? For that matter, what *was* sackcloth?

She bent her head against his chest and enjoyed the steadfast thud of a man marching after God's own heart. "Your mother has left a great deposit in you, Chance. Her legacy of faith is living here. The seeds she planted are sprouting up, and I must say it's beautiful. Your faith is like a garden, and every life around you is touched by the beauty."

He was silent for several seconds, then his chest quivered.

She looked up.

His cheeks looked about to explode. Her assessment was confirmed when laughter burst through his lips. "Sorry. It's just…you sounded like Ben when he's about to burst into poem or praise song."

She laughed with him, and it felt good. Better than anything in a long time.

"Yeah. The poet who uses flowery stuff—pun intended—to compose worship. You should pass along that whole garden concept to him. He could probably turn it into a song that would touch people."

"I will next time I see him."

"Which could be this Sunday in church."

Chloe nibbled her lip. "I'd like to try it. I'll see if Mom will go too."

"Then I'll invite Dad, because he hasn't been since Mom died. I have a feeling he'll go if he knows Mary is."

"I know it'll be hard for you to see him fall in love again."

"Not as hard as seeing him depressed and lonely and giving up on himself and life and all he loves to do."

She hugged him. "You're something else, Chance. What am I going to do with you?"

A shy blink. "Kiss me would be my first choice."

Chloe leaned back, shook her head and laughed.

"And laugh as long and as often as possible. You define gorgeous when you giggle." He smiled lopsidedly and still managed to look contrite. "Sorry. It's the waterfall's fault."

"It is quite romantic."

He grinned full-on, nothing shy in it. "I'm kidding, Chloe, sorta. What I meant to say earlier is that you can trust me. Trust God. Trust me. You have to choose to believe me when I say that I will do everything in my power to champion your dreams."

"What about your dreams, Chance? And what if they clash with mine and mine with yours?"

He grinned. "A divine detour never hurt anyone as far as I know. I'm willing to, as you say, recalculate my route. All I ask is that you be willing too. Are you?"

That was the hundred trillion dollar question.

Was she?

Chloe studied Chance and sent a silent plea heavenward. *God, I lay my plans at your feet. I accept Your will for my life even if it means the sifting of my dreams and enduring detours I didn't see coming.*

She slowly nodded her head.

Chapter Eighteen

Over the next month, Chance and Chloe settled into a regular dating routine. They grew even closer, and Chance was more than convinced that the day was coming soon when he could slide the diamond ring on her finger and let the world know she was his.

He was daydreaming about their future when his cell rang as he was working late at the DZ. He looked at the caller ID and punched the answer command. "Hey, Brock, what's up?"

"Uh, you need to meet me at Refuge's ER. Now!" A strangled sound came out of Brock.

"ER. What happened? You okay?"

Another strangled sound. "I am. But Chloe, she's not." A muted laugh blew forcefully through the phone.

"Shut up, Broccoli!" A strained female voice that sounded suspiciously like Chloe said from close by.

"Dude, what happened to her? What's so funny?"

"Treadmill mishap."

Chance bit back a grin. "What happened? She fall?"

"Big time. With Midnight's help. I've got the dog with me. He won't leave Chloe's side. She's hurt enough that I think she needs X-rays."

"Don't let her talk you out of it. How's Midnight? Is he hurt too?"

"Not unless Chloe gets a hold of him."

Chance laughed and headed to his car. "That means?"

"Apparently, the dog despises the treadmill. He tried to drag her off."

"Seriously?" Chance switched his phone to his hands-free device and pulled out of the driveway.

"She was running, and he kept barking and growling at the machine. She inclined it, and he went into a frenzy and yanked on her shoestring with his teeth. Trying to rescue her from it or something, I guess."

Chance stuffed some console change in his pockets for the hospital vending machine and listened intently to Brock relay the story. He imagined Chloe hurt too much to talk.

"She went down but tried to hold on. She's scraped up pretty good. Busted her lip. Ankle's possibly sprained too. We're gonna make sure it's not fractured. Looks terrible."

Ouch. Poor Chloe. "Sprains can look worse than breaks." He applied more gas and kept a safe eye out for other cars, namely Officer Stallings.

"That's what I told her. But being an OT, she

knows that. She also knew she was hurt enough she couldn't walk. She hopped down the boardwalk to my door, but I was out back helping Evie with something. Midnight led me to Chloe."

"Maybe he won't totally end up in the doghouse then." Chance laughed. "Pun intended. Good dog."

"Yeah, he's finally going to Evie so I can drive Chloe to the hospital. We'll meet you there."

"I'll call Mary to sit with Dad, then I'll be there."

"She's just going in for X-rays, then to Mary's because they're preparing paperwork to turn in to city hall. Why don't you and Ivan just meet us at Mary's."

"Sounds good. Thanks, Brock, for taking care of my woman."

Brock's grin echoed through the phone in the form of an amused exhale. "Sure."

"I'll return the favor when you fall through the hole into Wonderland and meet your Alice."

"You're pushin' it. Don't make me paint polka dots on your parachute."

Chance laughed. "Bye, Brock. Thanks."

A little while later, Mary met Chance and Ivan when they entered her foyer. "She's already here. They were able to do the X-rays quickly. She's feeling better, now that her ankle's wrapped and she knows it's just a sprain, but the doctor ordered her to stay off it for a while. She and Midnight will stay here for the next few days. You're welcome to sit with her, although she's pretty embarrassed and dreading the thought of seeing you."

Chance grinned. "I know exactly why."

"Because you told her so. She told me." Mary laughed and eyed the box of Chloe's favorite chocolates and the little stuffed Labrador puppy holding a silk rose in his paws. "But I have a feeling that adorable stuffed puppy will more than make up for any I-told-you-so."

"There'll be none of that from me, ma'am."

Mary chuckled and stepped outside with Ivan and Midnight. "I'm taking these two for their walk. Go on in. Second room to the right."

He knocked on Chloe's door. "Special delivery for a special girl."

A groan, then good-natured laughter floated toward him. "Hi, Hooligan number two. Come in. But don't dare say I told you so."

Chance came around the corner and smiled tenderly. "Hooligan number two?"

"Yes. Right now Midnight is Hooligan number one." She put a hand up to her swollen mouth. "I look terrible."

He sat on the edge of her bed. "You look beautiful."

Red rimmed her eyes and tissues littered her lap.

"You've been crying. Are you still in pain?"

She shook her head and drew a quivery breath. "I missed the town meeting today because of the fall. I called city hall but they don't want to reschedule because I was a no-show." He knew she'd stayed up for three solid days preparing for this crucial meeting, because he'd helped her and Mary brainstorm deep into the nights.

"Did you tell them why?"

She nodded. "Yes, but the person manning the phone was the very person most against this program."

"Steele." Anger surged.

"Yeah." Chloe looked close to bursting into tears again. "I feel like I'm pounding futile fists into rock walls. Maybe I'm not meant to start this kind of program down here."

"I don't believe that for a minute. Nor should you. Don't worry about city hall. I'll take care of it."

"How? Those people are impossible."

"Trust me, Chloe. I have clout."

"You'd go to bat for me?"

"In a heartbeat."

"Really? Even if they get a notion to form a crusty, brainless, two-pronged committee to fight you too?"

Chance laughed because her description of Refuge's stodgy mayor and lazy sheriff unfortunately fit.

"You bet. In the meantime, here's something to cheer you up." He pulled the goodies out from behind his back. "And tide me over until I can have real ones." He handed over the candy kisses.

She laughed and eyed the gifts. "You smart, sweet man! You brought chocolate and flowers."

He pulled the stuffed animal out next.

A sharp, happy gasp came out of her. "And a black Lab puppy!" She hugged it, then reached for Chance and gave him a python squeeze. "Thank you."

"You're welcome." He brushed a gentle thumb along her lip. "I'm sorry you got hurt."

Her expression grew wry.

"No, really, I am." He was. But at the same time the urge to laugh hit him out of nowhere.

He wouldn't laugh at her. He wouldn't.

His mouth twitched. He clenched his teeth. But images of Midnight trying to drag her from the evil treadmill's clutches chased him like a dog going after its own tail.

Her eyelids lowered. Pressure grew inside his cheeks. His face heated in effort to hold it in.

Chloe's hands went to her hips. "Go ahead. Get it out of your system."

Chance shook his head and pressed his lips together.

"Yes."

Chance brought his hand to his mouth and literally pinched it shut, then shook his head again.

"Stop that. You're gonna give yourself a hernia holding it in." She pulled his hand down.

A pent-up laugh whistled through.

She laughed too.

Until he opened his mouth.

"I love you, Chloe."

She froze and clutched the toy Lab close to her heart.

He laughed at her fearful expression, probably exacerbated by lack of sleep. "I'm not taking the pup back if you don't reciprocate. Take your time."

"Are you sure?" Her words swooped out, breathless.

"Never more."

"I—"

"Shhh," he whispered and pressed a petal to her lips. "I don't want you to say it back until you mean it."

"But—"

"After you've had a good night's sleep. I'd doubt otherwise."

"A man like you loves me." She stared at him for several long moments. Like she couldn't totally believe this was real. Her shoulders went droopy and her eyelids lowered. Chance directed her head to the pillow.

She was sawing logs before he got the covers tucked around her. The girl was downright exhausted.

She'd been awake seventy-two hours straight in an effort to convince Steele and Bunyan to give her program a chance, at least on a trial basis.

Enough was enough. Chance would see to it they saw things her way. He cared about Chloe, and everything she cared about had become important to him.

He'd gone with her to take Midnight to visit terminally ill kids as well as those in foster care due to abuse. He'd seen firsthand how much difference the dog could make. He saw how much joy the children and teens gave the dog too. A dog who'd grown up in horrific circumstances like themselves.

Chloe told him Midnight had been a bait dog for people arrested for dog fighting.

Chloe's program meant more animals would be rescued and more people would be uplifted by their loyalty and furry affection.

Chance was convinced God put dogs on the earth partly to demonstrate His steadfast, unconditional love.

The kind of love Chloe had needed from her father but never received. But if she said yes, he'd see to it the rest of her life was different. She would learn every day that a man's love for her could be trusted.

"I love you, sweetness," he whispered and stepped back to let her sleep.

I love you, sweetness.

What seemed a split second later, Chloe jolted awake. Bolted up in bed. "Did you mean it?"

Chance cracked a smile.

Facing her, he leaned back on the far end of her mom's guest bed and rested his body on his elbows. He stretched his long legs out in a slow recline as lazy and dizzying as the grin sliding across his face.

He stared, relaxed, unblinking, into her eyes and twirled the rose slowly between his fingers.

The man was mesmerizing.

According to the trademark lopsided grin creeping farther across his face, he knew it too.

Suddenly, she could see images of them married, and of him grinning lopsided in a dimly lit nursery while rocking a downy-haired baby, one with dual dimples and shy eyes and wrapped in a cartoon puppy bunting with neon-green trim.

She shook her head. "Staying up all night is for the birds." But for the life of her she couldn't stop staring at him and didn't care if he caught her gawking.

He leaned up and placed the soft rose between her eyes. "Get some sleep, Chloe." He ran the burgundy-petaled flower achingly slowly down her nose, following her facial curves until the flower fell softly against her lips. "See you in the morning, sweetness."

She breathed deeply of the scent of roses.

And of his love for the first time.

He removed the rose and replaced it with his lips, and she couldn't be sure which was softer.

"Sweet dreams."

Boy, would they ever be.

Chapter Nineteen

A wet nose bumped the back of her hand. Repeatedly. Chloe awakened. After the fatigue wore off enough to bring her bone-weary brain back to reality, panic kicked in.

She blinked, having no idea where she was.

Oh, right. Mom's house.

"Dog, you're acting psycho." Probably from missing her and his cuddle toys, which were back at the B&B.

Stress pressed her skull in a vice grip when she thought of Steele's unreasonable action over her missing the important meeting. Chloe swung her feet over the side.

The stuffed dog tumbled off the pillow beside her head.

And her heart remembered. Giddiness consumed her when Chance's declaration of love drifted across her soul.

It melted off most of the stress, but not all.

Chloe peered at her watch and gasped. She'd been due to meet legal counsel since she was going over city hall's belligerent balding heads.

Chance knocked, then walked in with food. His steps paused. "What's wrong?"

"I missed two vital meetings. One with Refuge City Hall, and one with my attorneys. Because our animal-assisted therapy program is considered a charity, our presence in court is mandatory. We go before the judge to present our case in a matter of days. We were to meet with attorneys today to prepare. I'm going to miss my deadline to get the zoning and tax paperwork in." She nibbled her lip.

He grinned.

She sat up. "What?"

"Mallory's in Refuge. She's at the meeting with the attorneys and CPA. Your mom's a proxy for you."

She blew a breath of relief. "What else?"

"There's no need to fret about the Refuge meeting either. You needed rest. I went on your behalf." He held an envelope in his hands.

A big, bulky envelope. He slipped a set of papers from it and unfolded them in front of her face.

Her eyes focused on the first sentence. "Congratulations…" She read a few more words and realized this letter meant her plans would go forth and that Refuge City Council had finally voted to approve her business.

"How did you pull this off?" She hugged—no, nearly strangled—him.

"Calm down and I'll tell you." Chance peeled her

arms from around his neck so he could see her face. "Mallory came down and gave me names of people your therapy animals have helped."

"She came because of my ankle sprain?"

He hesitated before answering. "Not totally. I'll let her share the rest with you."

"Okay." She hoped Mallory was okay. A horrible sinking sensation hit Chloe at the thought that Mallory had come to tell her she'd decided to step out of the program. That would mean Chloe's imminent return to Chicago.

"Ashleigh Petrowski traced the names Mallory provided, which scored us their numbers. I called the list and most let me record their testimonies of how much your program had helped them. Stallings pulled Steele into a back room and let him know that he had evidence Steele sleeps on the job. Steele buckled."

"What about Bunyan?"

"He was moved by the stories. He wants to meet Midnight and push funding your way."

Tears filled her eyes. "I don't know what to say. I'm quite frankly speechless."

And starting to realize more and more that he wouldn't hinder or dampen but help and champion her dreams.

"They've rescheduled the meeting for final decision, but I'll go with you in case Steele badgers you. That meeting will hopefully get your zoning in order, which will allow you to move forward with concrete plans."

"Thank you, Chance."

"My team's planning a big fundraising event to help get your therapy program off the ground here in Refuge. We're planning to host a festival."

She gasped. "You're for real?"

He nodded.

"Why are you doing all this for me?"

"I told you. I'm not settling for anything less than forever with you, Chloe. That means your program is my program. I won't ever keep you from your dreams, because your dreams will be my dreams too." He bent to kiss her on the forehead, but then pressed his forehead to hers and trailed a finger from her jawline to her chin, then lifted her face to his. "And as soon as you're better, I aim to claim that kiss that got away."

Her eyes widened. This man would not give up.

Thanks be to God.

"You need to call Mallory." Concern compressed Chance's lips.

Instantly, Chloe knew. "Something happened. Ash found something on Bert. Evidence of infidelity."

Chance chewed his lip and nodded. "I've said too much. Call her. She needs you." Chance stepped out as she dialed.

Chloe had a heart-to-heart with Mal who poured her hurt and anger out, then hung up because she had a rescue dispatch. Chance came back into the room. "Mal okay?"

"He bashed her heart, but at least her dreams will live."

He eyed her funny then. Apprehensively.

"Joel beeped in while I was talking to Mal. He's apparently joined the cupid posse."

Chance laughed. "What makes you say that?"

"He called to check on me, then launched into counsel mode."

"Sounds like Joel." Chance chuckled. "What'd he say?"

"Told me how you work with new recruits. Used the stories to convince me you'd come alongside me."

"That's true, Chloe."

"That's what we're about," she whispered, hoping to convince herself yet scared to believe and act on it.

He took her hand and brushed his finger along the length of her ring finger.

This time it was far from covert.

It left her breathless, as did the thought of a future with him and apprehension over his determination to pastor.

"That's what we'll always be about if you give us a chance. A good relationship is like rescue rope. It provides security and binds the other person in strength where they're weak. Brings them up when they can't lift themselves. It partners with gentle pulls. It never snaps apart the other's dreams."

He grasped her hand and grew as serious as she'd ever seen him. "Chloe?" He knelt!

For whatever reason, her eyes shot toward Dad's photo on the shelf behind Chance. Ironically, his kneeling put it in her direct line of sight.

Dad was standing in front of his church building.

Not once did he have his picture taken with Chloe. Not once. Panic and doubt swirled through and clutched her heart like a hand meant to strangle.

"Don't." Her heart thundered in her chest.

Please don't ask me for forever when I'm not sure I can offer tomorrow.

Yet another part of her heart, the one that used to be weak but was getting stronger, fell into frenzy to know.

What was he on the verge of asking?

What would she say?

Right now it was better left unsaid.

Just like holding back her *I love you* until she knew it could last for forever.

She just needed to be sure, sure, sure. Because she didn't want to string him along or let fear change her mind. This horrible fear that stalked her.

She studied him. His tender smile.

I'm not sure, but I think I love him.

He twisted to see what she stared at. His eyes softened. "Chloe, I may have an affinity for the church the same as your father, but I am not the same kind of man your father was. You have to choose to believe me."

"I want to," she whispered, trying very hard to tear her gaze off the photo and fix it on Jesus and Chance.

Don't let anything come along to change my mind.

Enter his world, she would. She was ready.

Chance started to step from the podium Sunday when Nolan rushed him like a suicide bomber.

"Dude, Chloe was here."

"What do you mean *was?* Church hasn't started yet."

"No, but she caught word about the announcement regarding you being officially ordained as a part-time youth pastor pending completed course work."

Chance scrubbed his hands over his face and left them there. "This isn't good." The first day she visits church, and it happens to be the day Rowan leaked official word.

Joel rapidly approached. "Chance, Chloe's outside. She fled from the church. Amber intercepted her. They're talking now."

Celia rushed up in an arm-flailing flurry. "Chance, Chloe was here. She left in tears. Go after her."

Now they were coming in twos. Mina and Sarah sped up. "Chloe came. She's very upset and—"

Chance nodded wryly. "I gathered that. Which way did she—"

Mina pointed in a direction. Celia shoved him there.

Chance found Rowan. "Dude, don't make the announcement yet. I need to talk to Chloe. I haven't told her today's the day."

Chance darted out the door and found Chloe and Amber beside the building. When Chloe saw him, she appeared to want to freeze and flee at the same time.

On approach, Chance nodded for Amber to go inside.

Praying, she mouthed as she passed, squeezing Chloe's shoulders in a sisterly hug.

Chance stepped close and braced his hands on Chloe's shoulders. She tensed, and his throat knotted like white pine.

"Chloe?"

"My whole life flashed in front of me in there, Chance. Memories of Mom cooking Dad Sunday dinner but he never showed up. Not even late. You can't imagine the hard work, then heartache on her face when week after week he didn't return for the dinners she cooked, even though he promised."

"Chloe, I'm sorry."

"He had to stay late and pray with people, he said. For women who felt neglected by their husbands. Do you know what it's like to live gut-wrenchingly lonely within a marriage, Chance?" Anger flashed in her eyes.

"No. You know I've never been married."

"Neither have I, but I saw my mom live that scenario day after day and I don't want to endure it."

He swallowed. Grasped her hands. "Chloe, you won't."

She glared at the building again. "Do you know how hard it was for me to show up here today? Coming to church feels like facing my father's longtime mistress." She gave a self-deprecating laugh.

He rubbed circular, calming motions into her thumbs.

"I vowed that I'd never marry someone whose

career would cause me to set aside my dreams. And I especially promised myself I'd never marry a pastor. Then I get here and find out you'll be ordained today?"

"Chloe, how your dad went about things wasn't right. A man's family ought to be first. I'm not your dad. I'm nothing like that."

Chloe laughed but without humor. "The absolute last thing I want to be is a pastor's wife. When did you plan to tell me, Chance? I had to come and hear it from strangers."

"I'm sorry you found out that way. What did you hear?"

"When Rowan met me, the first thing he said was he thinks you'll make a great part-time youth pastor, starting today. That was my first clue. So like an idiot I blurted, "Pastor? *Today?*"

Chance stayed silent, knowing she needed to vent it out of her system. She knew he was getting ordained but probably assumed she'd have time to get used to the idea.

"The church waived its policy and offered immediate honorary pastoral ordination since we're already mentoring in the community. I only recently found out."

"Rowan realized I hadn't come here to show my support of you. I showed up unknowing. He apologized and said he's surprised you didn't tell me. Guess what, Chance? I'm surprised too."

"I apologize. But in my mind, ordination is only a formality. I didn't think about it because titles don't mean anything to me. You know I work with youth. But the association over this church requires anyone in that level of leadership to go through the motions of ordination."

"How long have you known?"

"Two days."

Her face instantly softened. "What does it entail? A lot of time?"

"Not really. I plan to do a satellite course here at the church on Tuesdays with Rowan in order to be ordained as a youth minister."

Though his tone was reassuring, the *minister* word rushed through her like a verbal tornado, whirling her thoughts. Chloe fought to stay non-judgmental. On the other hand, rebellious thoughts ran around her brain at will.

Not only was Chance volunteering heavily, three days a week so far, he was going to become a pastor. He told her PJs retire early. So he'd go from being a PJ to a pastor?

A sinking feeling hit her in the heart and gut. Slowly but surely he was adding things to the time-table of his day that would slowly snuff out time with her.

As if sensing the epic battle raging in her head, Chance stepped closer and strengthened his grip. "I already volunteer. Rowan joined the National Guard. He just needs a couple of backups to substitute for him once a month."

"How long?"

"The course takes less than a year."

"What if he gets deployed? What then?"

"Then the church hires another full-time youth pastor, and soldiers overseas will benefit from Rowan's influence."

Something pecked at her not to make more of this than it was. But she still felt betrayed. Horribly betrayed.

"I planned this before I met you, Chloe. This isn't some new thing I pulled out of my ear. I just didn't think to mention it to you with everything in the last two days. In fact, we forgot it was today until Rowan reminded us."

"Us?"

"Yeah. Vince is taking the course with me. He and I will alternate subbing for Rowan to ease the burden on both of us. Come in for the meeting, Chloe. See what it's about."

Thoughts still flew around like arrows, and anger still quivered her insides…to the point her fingers trembled.

Though fear-driven emotions flailed against it, her good sense told her to grant him the benefit of the doubt. Still, fear resided.

Should she trust her emotions? Or trust Chance? Because right now, it couldn't be both.

Please help me see, Jesus. I want to believe the truth. And I want to be free of the pain of my past.

She sighed. "Don't get me wrong, Chance. I'm fairly independent and certainly no codependent clingy vine. But how can I be sure this won't be one more thing pulling you away from me emotionally or using up our time?"

"Because I told you we're about partnership. You could share it with me."

"I'm not qualified to work with youth."

"Really? You could have fooled me. I watch you interact with teens at the PJ cookouts. There are a lot of lonely girls who feel neglected and abandoned by their fathers in that group. They need to connect with someone who's been there."

"Chance, as much as I wish I could help them, I can't. That would make me have to go back there in my mind, to that painful place, and I just can't." But her gaze veered toward two of the girls who'd stepped outside for some air.

Her heart wanted to reach out, grab and hug them.

Maybe this church was different. Maybe she could trust. Engage herself in it. But that would mean putting herself out there in a place of risk to be hurt again.

"Chance, I-I'm trying. But I just, I don't know."

He dropped his head. "Chloe, I'll give it up for you. If that's what you want, I won't work with youth. I won't be ordained." He looked pained to say it.

Guilt slashed through her, especially when she saw teen faces pressed in the window, faces of souls lost and needing an adult's love, guidance and acceptance so badly.

"And my PJ team, we're not on missions often. We have training ops every other weekend. Missions rarely last longer than two weeks. I'll be home more than I'm gone. You could sit with me when I work out. Most of what I do, you could tag along." Now that got her attention.

"I could watch you work out?" Her cheeks tinged. "Now that sounds appealing."

He laughed. "At least I know we have attraction going for us. That's important."

"But it's not all."

"We have more going for us, Chloe. When two people love each other, they're willing to work the roadblocks out of their relationships."

"Who said anything about love?"

He bent close. "You don't have to. I can read you like a book."

How could he know she loved him? She wasn't even certain herself until last night.

The very nature of his PJ creed meant he'd put his career before personal duties or desires.

Did that mean family?

And would he apply his PJ creed to his pastoring?

"Do you really love me enough not to be a pastor?"

His smile faded, and he brushed a tender gaze down her face. "I love you too much to let you get away for any reason."

"You make me sound like the big one that you can't get a hook into."

"Hey, if it were only as easy as setting a hook in you and reeling you in, I'd be a happy man."

She laughed and rubbed her arms in effort to ignore the new drove of teens pressing their faces in the window.

"You're a tough nut to crack, Chloe Callett. But my

love for you is tougher. And as much as I'd love to stand out here and kiss you all morning, I'm set to speak. It's too late to have someone cover for me. I need to get in there." His face was almost apologetic as he bent and kissed her cheek, then slipped from her presence and toward the entrance to the youth room.

He turned once and looked at her with an expression that left no doubt he loved her.

And he didn't seem upset that she hadn't said it back.

But she did. She did love him back. So much it ached to watch him walk away.

Steadfast love. Long-suffering love.

She didn't want this magnificent man to ever know what unrequited love feels like.

She'd lived that in her childhood.

In that moment she knew that Chance's love for her, his treatment of her and their relationship, was way different than her father's treatment. And she knew now without a doubt that she loved him back.

She also knew Chance wanted her to go inside the church with him but didn't want to push. Something inside her now wanted to love him and stand beside him anywhere as long as they had years together. The feeling intensified, and she realized she was even willing to give up her own dreams for the gift of this man's love. She loved her plans for animal-assisted therapy, yet how much more important were people than animals?

Her gaze veered toward the glass, where youth romped around the room.

How many of them felt ignored, abandoned, unloved?

And how many of them would be rescued from despair, loneliness, unworthiness and the depressing fate of a dead-end life when they learned the truth through Chance? The truth that they were never absent from God's sight, never far from His good thoughts toward them, never out from underneath the umbrella of His love and always, no matter how they felt, tucked safely in the Refuge of his wings.

How many of them would grow up not knowing it if Chance chose not to pursue the youth pastor position?

Chloe couldn't do that to them. She couldn't let that happen.

She knew he was meant to do this.

She knew she was meant to help him.

Those children were meant to know their Father loved them.

That had always been Chloe's refuge in her storm of loneliness. The concept of Daddy God. That her earthly father was a temporary model, and her father in Heaven was her real dad. There was never a doubt that He loved her.

If she had that much to give, that small slice of knowledge of God's sustaining love and affection toward her, she must share it with the teen girls whose hearts so desperately cried out for a father's affection.

Unlike God, every man's love had a breaking point.

She suddenly didn't want Chance to go another second without knowing how she felt.

Unlike her dad, she would not withhold her affection.

Chloe rushed across the asphalt.

Chance paused at the door and turned in time to catch her when she flung herself into his arms, out of sight of the teens. Rowan, who'd had his hand on Chance's shoulder, smiled and stepped back. Chloe blushed when she realized she'd interrupted Rowan praying privately for Chance.

"I'm sorry." She started to step away.

Chance pulled her back and grinned at Rowan.

Rowan waved. "We were just wrapping up."

Chloe clung to Chance's neck and hugged as tightly as she could. Patient but looking a little confused, Chance patted her back and held her several long moments before leaning his head back. "What's this all about, Chloe?"

With him peering down at her, she wished she could give him that kiss now. She grinned at the thought. In due time. "I love you too, you big doofus."

His arms tightened around her, as if he were holding on for dear life. Before she knew what hit her, his lips were brushing hers in a tender kiss. His eyes were tentative as he pulled away. "Does that hurt?"

"I'm not sure. Try it again, and I'll pay more attention this time," she murmured while wrapping her hand around the back of his neck and pulling him in for another sweet kiss.

Gentle. The man was everything she could hope for. And the kiss was even better than the last.

She wished she could kiss him all day, but then she'd pay for it later and she was almost out of ibuprofin and, well, they were standing in front of a room with impressionable youth who could bop out the door any moment.

"God will be with us, Chloe. Okay?"

She nodded into his chest and relished the feeling of loving and being loved. Of knowing she didn't have to do a single thing to gain his attention except exist. That Chance loved her for her and she didn't have to strive an ounce to earn his affection.

Through his time, his patience, his honorable hugs and sweetly murmured words, he had assured and reassured her of his devotion and steadfast love.

He gave it freely, and she drank it in like a woman whose soul had spent its life dying of thirst.

She was thirsty no more.

Chapter Twenty

"Hey, guys. I'd like you to meet someone special. This is Chloe." Chance tugged her toward the gangly group of teens once they returned inside a couple of kisses later.

Teens lined every inch of the room. Popular kids, misfits and those on the fringe. Chloe was sure there were brainiacs and some who were slower. Some were bookish, a few bored. Still others were tattooed or pierced. There were athletes and preps, punks and emo. Even a few goths and retro rockers.

Yet one common thing resided in their young eyes when Chance waltzed her around the room.

Respect. It gleamed from every teen to Chance as he greeted them with handshakes and affectionate high fives on his way to the camouflage-patterned podium.

The need for acceptance trailed it. No matter what walk of life these kids came from or what color their skin was or what side of the tracks their families originated from, they all wanted and needed love, a sense of belonging and unconditional acceptance.

It only took her three minutes to figure out they had found that in Chance as well as Jesus, and that Chance, like Jesus, loved these kids with his whole being.

After Chance delivered a dynamic message, the girls clustered around Chloe like petals to the center of a flower. A quick head count told her there were far more girls than boys and not near enough help. Even with the PJs' wives helping out, not all of the girls would be able to connect one-on-one or open up individually.

All at once, Chloe knew her calling was to come alongside Chance and partner with him in reaching out to these youth. She would be forced to step boldly past her fears and out of the clutches of her painful childhood.

With every passing minute she spent in the youth room for Sunday school, her compassion grew and pulsed through her until she felt bulldozed by it, but in a good way.

"I want you to go through with it, Chance," she said firmly as the group filed from the Sunday school room to the auditorium for the church service.

He faced her and raised his eyebrows.

"The ordination. These kids need you. Need us."

Their eyes connected. Held.

"You're sure about this?" He inclined his head.

She grinned. "As sure as you were that God would somehow work things out so you could do both—be with me and work with them too, despite the fact that you said you wouldn't if I didn't want you to."

He laughed. "How did you know I prayed that?"

"Because He answered your prayer by reassuring me." She steered him toward the stage. "Let's go. Rowan, and your destiny in planting hope in the hearts of these kids regarding their futures, are both eagerly awaiting you."

Chloe took a front-row seat.

Vince Reardon and a lovely pixie-haired woman took the seats beside her. "Hi, Chloe. This is my wife, Val."

Val sat next to Chloe and shook her hand. "Pleased to finally meet you. I feel like I know you from Chance's stories of you."

"Don't believe a word of them." Chloe laughed and hoped she didn't sound as giddy as she felt over the fact that Chance talked about her often to his friends.

"Rowan mentioned he thought your rescued animals would be good therapy for teens. Especially those in counseling for abuse," Val said when Vince joined Chance.

"Are there many in the group?"

Val paused. "More than you'd ever guess."

Suddenly, Chloe caught glimpses of her and Chance's gifts merging into one common path.

That moment, he turned and caught her staring. His explosive grin rippled joy and elation through her.

And Chloe felt the peace that passes all understanding. Nope, she didn't understand why Chance loved her so much, but she was sure glad he did.

"I don't believe this." Chloe unclenched her fists as she stood on the property she had planned to buy for the program. "It was just up for sale."

Mallory, down for the weekend, eyed the land Chance had shown Chloe the day of their four-wheeler ride. "It would have been a perfect spot for our facilities too."

Disappointment sliced through Chloe with each blink toward the Sold sign. "Let's go. Sorry to have dragged you all the way out here for nothing."

"It's not for nothing, Chloe. I needed to get away after breaking up with Bert. And I have more news."

Chloe's heart fluttered at Mallory's grin. "Tell me."

"I might be able to finish school down here. My credits will transfer. We just have to talk our supers into letting us open the Refuge clinic first."

Elation filled Chloe at the prospect.

"Let's head back. Chance is expecting you, and this is one time you don't want to be late." Mallory bit her lip and headed toward Chloe's car, parked near the road.

"You should go skydiving with us, Mal. My first time won't be the same without you."

"Trust me, you'll want to make this jump alone."

Chloe shrugged and pulled onto the road headed toward the DZ where Chance had scheduled a tandem skydive with her.

When Chloe arrived at the DZ, Mallory walked inside after instructing Chloe to wait here. Chance met Chloe at the car with a gift box adorned in neon-green silk ribbon.

"For me?"

He nodded and grinned as she tugged the end of the ribbon. Exiting, she slid the lid off and pulled the material out. "A skydiving outfit in neon-green!" She clutched it to herself and hugged him.

He held her to him and didn't seem to want to let go. His Adam's apple bobbed above her head. She tilted back. "You seem nervous. Is it because I'm sky-diving with you?"

He grinned. "N-no. That's not it." He whistled, and she wondered why his stutter had resurfaced. If he wasn't nervous, was he stressed about something?

Midnight barreled around the building. Chance made a command. Midnight walked up and nudged her palm as if to be petted.

"Open your hand," Chance instructed.

Her heart pounded as she did so. Chance nodded at Midnight, and the dog dropped an envelope in her hand.

Her fingers shook as she opened it. "A deed…to that land." Chloe lifted her eyes to Chance but could hardly see him past the moisture that suddenly filled them. She rushed him, hugging with all her might. "You are the one who bought it?"

"With help from my team. We all pitched in."

"But why would you do something so extravagant?"

"Because I love you and I'll do whatever's necessary to show you that I aim to back your dreams with my whole heart. And even my wallet. And my friends' wallets, for that matter." He grinned.

"Oh, Chance. I don't know what to say other than thanks, and that seems too miniscule." She blinked tears back and hugged him again.

"There's more." He nodded to the other envelope.

She tugged out a notecard that read, "Look on Midnight's collar."

Chloe knelt and reached for it. A filmy neon-green satchel hung near his tags. It held another tag.

Wait. Something sparkled when a sunbeam caught it.

She leaned in.

It was no tag.

She grasped it. "A ring?"

He grinned.

She tried to open the satchel but her fingers quaked. "Oh! That looks suspiciously like a diamond."

He chuckled and unhooked the little bag. Mallory returned and took the dog then disappeared quickly. Chance tugged the string and pulled out the prettiest ring she'd ever set eyes on. "I'm afraid to ask what this is because I'm scared it's not."

He took her hand. "Go change. I'll meet you at the plane."

Chloe dressed faster than ever before. She wondered where Mallory went. She'd know what was going on. Whether this was just a promise ring or the real thing. Her heart pounded at the possibilities.

The small aircraft taxied to the pick-up point. Chance led her out to meet it. "You remember the positioning and landing techniques?"

"Yep. I paid attention to my very cute teacher." Goggled, she grinned and hurried her steps toward the plane. She wasn't one ounce scared.

Once they were airborne and circling the area between the B&B and the DZ, Chloe saw it immediately.

The plane circled the B&B three times.

On the roof, waving like a flag of surrender in white were the words, Marry Me, Chloe?

She rested her head back on strong shoulders. "You really mean this?"

"I do."

"Then so do I!"

"You do?"

"I do!"

Chance grinned. "Then remember that phrase."

Her insides exploded with joy. She regarded his face with wonder, then eyed the ground and the vast expanse of sky the same way.

He checked his altimeter. "Ready?"

"Never have I been more ready for anything."

"That's my girl. Okay, sweetness, it's time. Let's go."

They moved toward the passageway as one, knowing this was just the beginning of a thrill-filled life where seasons and dreams were uncertain, but

Chloe finally certain that with God's help they'd weather the path together.

She knew that Chance's purchasing that property had broken any remaining doubt in her mind about his commitment to helping her program.

What was important to her had become important to him. She thought of the teens and realized the same was true for her.

"Yes, Chance! A million times over."

He grinned. "You're sure?"

"Definitely! I want to marry you, Chance, and I'll even have babies as soon as you're ready."

He laughed. "What if I want to get started on our honeymoon?"

Despite the cold air at high altitude, she blushed.

His face gleamed with that lovable lopsided grin. "We'll make a great team as parents. I can't wait to see you grow into the mom I know you're meant to be."

Chance nodded to the pilot, then guided them into the true-blue arms of a familiar but unchartered sky.

Blasting wind caught then carried them in its measureless embrace.

"Whaaaaaaaa!" Chloe wobbled beneath him. She felt the raw panic of first-time free fall sheer through her.

Calm replaced it as Chance reached for her arms and guided them alongside his, reminding her of their proper place and safe position.

She relaxed and let her arms rest against his in free-fall mode.

Exhilarating.

At the right time, he tugged their parachute cord. It plumed open. They slowed and the howling ceased.

His "Marry Me, Chloe?" grew larger the closer they got to the ground. Her loudly proclaimed answer resonated.

Yes.

Yes!

Their feet touched solid earth as one unit, symbolizing to her their leap of faith, not only into each other's hearts, but also into an unknown forever.

Chloe turned and hugged him. "That was an absolute blast! It went *so* fast. I can't believe it's over!"

Chance captured her and that elusive kiss. "*Au contraire*, my bright-green bundle of talkative, chocolate-loving sweetness. That was only the beginning."

* * * * *

Dear Reader,

This book was about partnership, romance and reaching out. I pray that you have people in your life who both pray you through hard seasons and prod you along when you need a good boot to the caboose. I'm thankful for a group of writers who banded together when we were all unpublished and making the finals of writing contests together. We determined to pray and prod and challenge and encourage one another to publication. To date, all but a few of the fifteen of us have publishing contracts. If you are an aspiring author or you simply love to be entertained by warm, funny women, visit our blog at www.seekerville.blogspot.com.

I love hearing from readers. I invite you to e-mail me at Cheryl@CherylWyatt.com or write me at PO Box 2955, Carbondale, IL 62902-2955.

If you'd like new-release news and goodies exclusive to subscribers, sign up for my quarterly newsletter by visiting my Web site, www.cherylwyatt.com, and entering your e-mail address in the space provided. I respect your privacy and won't share your info with a third party.

Warm thanks for taking the time to read my book. Blessings to you and your family. May you have a strong sense of God's steadfast love and presence.

Cheryl Wyatt

QUESTIONS FOR DISCUSSION

1. Why do you think Rowan thought Chance would make a good part-time youth pastor?

2. Could you understand Chloe's reticence for romance? Why or why not?

3. Do you think Mallory and Brock would make an interesting romantic pair? Why or why not?

4. How do you think Chance's mom's faith played a part in his steadfast character?

5. Did you feel Ivan fell in love again too soon? Why or why not?

6. In what ways do you think Chloe's animals help rehabilitate humans?

7. Do you agree with Mary and Ivan dating? Please discuss.

8. Could you empathize with Ivan losing his will to live after losing his wife and his mobility? If so, how so?

9. Chance said he thinks everyone needs a Chloe in their life. Who do you have in your life that's always upbeat and brings up others? Discuss.

10. Do you blame Mallory for not seeing sooner her fiancé's true colors? Why or why not?

11. How did it make you feel to know that Chloe rescues abused animals and gives their lives meaning and purpose?

12. Could you understand Chance wanting a family while he's young? Do you think his wishes were unreasonable?

13. What do you think bonds Chance's Pararescue Jumper (PJ) team?

14. Do you think God brought Chance and Chloe together in this story? Why or why not?

15. How do you think Midnight will respond to a pot-bellied pig on his turf?

Love Inspired®
SUSPENSE
RIVETING INSPIRATIONAL ROMANCE

Watch for our new series of
edge-of-your-seat suspense novels.
These contemporary tales
of intrigue and romance
feature Christian characters
facing challenges to their faith...
and their lives!

NOW AVAILABLE IN REGULAR
& LARGER-PRINT FORMATS

Steeple
Hill®

Visit:
www.SteepleHill.com